Hetty's Hut

- HELEN CLARKE & SARAH CONACHER-

An environmentally friendly book printed and bound in England by
www.printondemand-worldwide.com

This book is made entirely of chain-of-custody materials

www.fast-print.net/store.php

Hetty's Hut
Copyright © Helen Clarke/Sarah Conacher 2014

A catalogue record for this book is available from the British Library

ISBN 978-178035-780-5

First published 2014 by
FASTPRINT PUBLISHING
Peterborough, England.

Dedication

This is dedicated to our families and friends who have supported us throughout. To Duncan, Christopher, Rachael, Graham, Ross and James with love. We have thoroughly enjoyed creating Hetty's Hut and we thank Sally Kealy for her initial input and Hilary Ball for her amazing artwork.

Chapter 1

Hetty Webster looked around the dining table at the grown-ups who were busy unwrapping their fish and chips; they all looked a bit worried and Hetty wasn't sure if that meant that she should be worried as well. She decided to postpone worrying till she'd eaten her fish and chips; she couldn't remember the last time she'd been allowed to eat anything like it. Mum simply didn't approve of anything being fried or bought from a take-away. Hetty felt really naughty as she unwrapped the paper and smelt the delicious chips and the golden crispy fish. She couldn't wait any longer and chose a particularly delicious looking chip and bit into it; it was quite simply the best thing she'd tasted for ages.

"Would you like ketchup Poppet?"

Gran reached across with the bottle.

"There you are, can you manage?"

"Thanks Gran, this is lovely."

Hetty dipped the next chip into the puddle of ruby red sauce and greedily ate it, licking her fingers noisily, savouring every bit. She kept expecting someone to tell her to use a knife and fork, as Mum would have done but no one did. Fingers came first, she thought and carried on.

Hetty was really looking forward to living closer to Gran and Grandpa again; she'd missed being able to see them every weekend whilst she had been living in the city for the last two years.

Hetty was also looking forward to meeting up with her old friends that she had known when she was at primary school here. She had seen one or two of them when they'd visited Gran and Grandpa but she really hoped that she would be able to make friends with them again. This summer she and Dad were moving back to the seaside town where his parents lived whilst Mum and Hetty's brother Ollie, were staying in the city flat above Mum's posh dress shop. Only problem was Dad had discovered that afternoon that he and Hetty couldn't move into their new house just yet and so they were homeless. That explained the worried looks around the table. Hetty thought that they could stay the night with Gran and Grandpa but their bungalow was very small. She was really hoping that Dad wouldn't decide to send her back to live with Mum and Ollie for the summer; the thought of being cooped up in a two bedroomed flat above a shop, with no garden and, oh no, horror of horrors... she'd have to share a bedroom with Ollie!

Everyone was finishing their fish and chips but still looked worried.

"What's going to happen Dad? Will I have to go back to Mum's, cos I really don't want to share a room with

Ollie?" Hetty asked the question in a quiet voice not really wanting to hear the answer.

"I really don't know just yet sweetheart but try not to worry about it; it's getting late so you need to get ready for bed, give me a shout when you're ready and I'll come and tuck you in."

Dad winked at her as he helped to clear the wrappers away; he sounded a lot more cheerful than he looked but Hetty was sure he would sort something out.

Gran and Grandpa's house was a sort of bungalow; it had one big bedroom downstairs for them, with a specially designed bathroom and lots of room for Grandpa's wheelchair to move about in, which made it easier for Gran to look after him. There was a special hoist above the bed to lift him in and out of his chair and bed. Hetty was allowed to play in it some times and hung around above the bed whilst Gran changed the sheets; she couldn't imagine what it must be like to have to always get in and out of bed like that.

As Hetty walked past the bedroom she got the feeling that she wouldn't be having a lift in the hoist tonight. At the end of the corridor was a flight of stairs that led to another small bedroom that had been created in the loft space. Hetty's grandparents had had it made when the children were small so that Hetty and Ollie could stay with them on the evenings when they were on babysitting duty.

Upstairs, under the eaves, was a single bed that had another bed, which slid out from underneath it to make a second, smaller bed. There wasn't a lot of space in the room but it was fine for the odd night now and again.

Dad had unrolled Hetty's sleeping bag and put out her pyjamas next to Flopsy, her pink bunny. Hetty changed quickly into her nightclothes and ran downstairs to wash. As she cleaned her teeth she looked at her reflection. Could she really be bothered to try to untangle her mass of curly blonde hair? Surely nobody would notice tonight.

On her way back upstairs she put her head around the living room door.

"Night, night, Gran, Grandpa."

Hetty went over to them both for a kiss and a hug

"Don't worry Poppet, we'll think of something," Grandpa said as he hugged her., "Sleep tight, see you in the morning."

"OK, up you go then." Dad got up to take her up the stairs and as she wriggled into her sleeping bag he tried to reassure her again.

"It will be fine I'm sure. See you in the morning, kiss, kiss." Dad shut the door and Hetty heard his footsteps as they retreated down the stairs.

Hetty wasn't sure how long she'd been asleep, but she knew what had woken her up – loud voices. Dad and Gran were arguing about something. She couldn't quite make out the words so she quietly got out of bed and eased the door open and sat on the top step to listen.

"It's no good. We just can't help you; there isn't enough room here. You should have thought of this before you decided to leave her. Why you couldn't have stayed together, I really don't know; it didn't happen in our day., The children came first and we stayed together whatever the problems were."

Gran sounded angrier than Hetty had ever heard her before. Hetty had a sick feeling in her tummy, she hugged

Flopsy close and closed her eyes to stop the tears which were threatening, making her eyes ache.

Whatever was Dad going to say to her? It had been bad enough sitting on the stairs in their house, just like she was doing now, listening to Mum and Dad argue in the previous few months, but she had really thought that it was all going to be OK from now on. Her ears caught the sound of Dad sighing; he sounded sad as he replied.

"I know we can't stay Mum, so don't feel bad. If the worst comes to the worst then Hetty will have to go back to Amanda and Ollie, although there isn't really enough room there either and perhaps I could go and stay with Tim." (Tim was Dad's best friend and taught at the same school as Dad.)

"Hopefully it won't be for long;, when the builder gets back from his holiday he's promised it would be a priority to sort us out. It's Hetty I worry about, she so needed this summer with a bit of stability after all the upset and stress of the last few months."

"Not to mention the strain you've been under," said Gran.

Hetty heard Dad let out a great sigh.

"Well, I'm going to sleep on it, Mum. Do you need me to do anything?"

Hetty heard Dad getting up, so she quickly slipped back into bed and pretended to be asleep when he tiptoed into the small room a few minutes later.

Next morning Hetty woke up early; she wriggled out of her sleeping bag, trying not to disturb Dad and went downstairs to the bathroom. When she came out Gran was in the kitchen making tea.

"Here you are Poppet. Take a cup of tea up to Dad; would you like a cup?"

"No thanks Gran, could I have some juice please?"

Hetty carefully carried the tea up to Dad who was just waking up.

"Thanks Hetty," he said rubbing his eyes and yawning. "Did you sleep OK?"

"Not too bad thanks, what about you?" Dad didn't look as if he'd slept much but he smiled at her, stretched and said, "Yes thanks, best get up and see what we can sort out."

Hetty and Dad washed, dressed and got the breakfast ready whilst Gran sorted herself out and got Grandpa ready for the day.

Eventually they were all seated at the breakfast table. It looked as though Gran hadn't slept much either and everyone was very quiet until Grandpa suddenly spoke up.

"I've had an idea," he said, pausing to look around to see the effect his words would have. "What about staying in the beach hut? Some people stay there for the whole summer, you know."

There was a stunned silence for a minute or two and then Hetty exploded with excitement as she realised what Grandpa was suggesting.

"Wow Grandpa, what an epic idea! Oh Dad, can we...? Please, please! Staying there would be sooooo much fun."

Hetty suddenly felt as though a huge worry had gone, she could stay with Dad all summer and oh, it would be great and best of all, no sharing a room with Ollie.

"Hang on a minute, don't get carried away." Gran brought her down to earth. "I don't know, we haven't used the hut for ages, it must be five years at least. We left some things there and the rest is in the garage but I don't know what state it will be in."

"I always knew that your aversion to throwing things away would come in useful one day." Dad joked, smiling broadly at Gran.

Hetty grinned; it was the first time Dad had looked happy since they got there yesterday afternoon.

"Did you sleep there when you were a boy, Dad?" Hetty asked.

"Yes, we used to spend the whole summer there and it was always sunny and never rained. Auntie Jenny and I would be out exploring and having adventures all day, we had a whole gang of friends and we just had fun all day and every day. Your Gran never knew what we were up to," Dad laughed as he remembered his childhood summers. "I can't wait to see it again."

"I remember going there I think," said Hetty. "There was a lot of sand and the sea was all around, we went on a little train to get there and there were lots of other little huts in the sand dunes. Mum didn't like the sand because her high heels kept sinking."

The memory of her Mum tottering around trying to stay upright made her smile.

"That's right Hetty, what else do you remember?" Dad asked.

"Well, I remember a little ladder inside the hut, going up to a platform where there was a bedroom. Will I be able to sleep up there?"

Hetty was so excited she didn't wait for the reply.

"And there was a little kitchen at the back and a veranda at the front with steps leading down to the sand.

I remember having picnics, Ollie and Mum were always moaning about the sand getting everywhere."

"Well," said Grandpa, "I did try to keep it in good order before I got stuck in this silly wheelchair, it'll be good to have the old place opened up and used again."

Grandpa looked a bit sad and Hetty got up and gave him a hug.

"Perhaps we can get you down there when we've checked it out; there will be three of us to help and I'm really strong you know."

Hetty hated it when he had to miss out on things because of his wheelchair and secretly determined that she would get him there somehow, whatever it took.

"Well, that would be great," said Grandpa, looking a lot more cheerful. "It sounds as though it's all decided then."

After breakfast Hetty and Dad set off in Dad's car to the car park at the quayside, opposite the sandy spit where a number of colourful beach huts could be seen nestling amongst the golden sand dunes. They parked and walked over to the harbour's edge to wait for the ferry to take them across the water to the little community of huts.

Just before they had left, Gran had found the key and had given it to Dad, reminding him how to find the hut.

"When you get off the ferry, turn left and then after about fifty metres you'll see the shower block. The hut is number 65 and is set back, just to the right of the main pathway. I do hope it's all OK, I wish it was me going to live there, what fun you'll have! See you later; I'm going to sort out the garage and find some of the other bits you will need." She waved them off as she turned towards the garage.

The ferry was just pulling in to the quayside; Hetty was dancing about, hopping from one foot to the other. In all her eleven years she could never remember being so excited. What would her friends say when they found out that she was going to live in a beach hut for the whole summer?

Chapter 2

At around the same time that Hetty was eating her fish and chips on Friday evening, Charlie Parsons sat and looked around the table in the beach hut that belonged to his grandparents. His family was sitting together inside the hut, as it was a cool evening now that the heat from the sun had gone. All that remained of the barbeque that the family had just enjoyed was a couple of sausages and a lonely bread roll. Mum, Dad, Grandad and Nana were enjoying a cup of coffee and Charlie's little sister Lucy was curled up on Mum's lap sucking her thumb, with her doll, Ruby under her arm.

Charlie knew that it was almost time to say goodbye to Mum and Dad and he could tell that Lucy was going to make a huge fuss when the time came for them to go. He was going to be really cool and not let them know that he would miss them, after all he was nearly thirteen and showing that you miss your parents was just so pathetic. Even though they were going to be away for a month Charlie would be fine, he was sure. Mum was much better now; the cruise they were about to go on was a celebration of the fact that she had been given the all-clear, after having had a year of treatment. Charlie didn't know exactly what had been wrong with Mum, but he knew it had been serious. It had been a frightening time, so staying in a beach hut without Mum and Dad for a month of the summer holidays would be a piece of cake. Staying with Nana and Grandad would be fine as Charlie knew just how to wrap them around his little finger; after all, he was the first grandchild and they truly believed that he could do no wrong.

Lucy was a different matter. In fact, she was his main concern. How was he going to avoid her following him around and trying to go with him wherever he went? He hoped he wouldn't have to look after her all the time. He hated having her tagging along with him; that really wasn't cool. In fact girls weren't cool, full stop! Not for the first time he wished that she had been a boy, a little brother would have been so much fun, they really would have had a good time together, playing football, tennis and cricket, going fishing and exploring; the list was endless. Instead of that, he had a stupid sister who seemed to cry all the time and couldn't catch, hit, throw or kick a ball to save her life. Charlie hoped all his mates from last year would arrive soon; maybe he could persuade some of the girls to play with Lucy and let him off the hook.

"Charlie darling, we're just off." Mum was looking down at him expectantly; he had been miles away, lost in thought. "Now make sure you help Nana, look after Lucy and help with the jobs that need doing in the hut. You can make a start by washing up the supper things." Charlie turned away and closed his eyes so that Mum couldn't see how close he was to tears.

He took a deep breath. "Of course I will Mum; I hope you have a lovely holiday." Charlie smiled bravely.

"Oh, he's such a good boy. He'll be a great help, won't you Charlie?" Nana ruffled his hair and tried to hug him. With a neat side-step, Charlie avoided her outstretched arms and jumped down the beach hut steps onto the sand.

"I'll walk to the ferry with you Dad." Charlie reckoned that, with a bit of luck, he could have a bit of time on his own on the way back.

Nana was giving Mum a big hug. "We'll be fine, now off you go and enjoy the cruise, we'll be here when you get back; you deserve to have some fun."

Nana turned away to wipe her eyes and, holding her hand out, she said, "Come along Lucy, let's go to wave them off."

Obediently, Lucy jumped down from the chair and gave Mum and Dad a kiss. She looked as if she might start to cry as well but Dad picked her up and swung her around and she started to giggle, tears forgotten. Thank goodness, because when she started to cry it was ear splitting and Charlie hated it.

Much to Charlie's dismay it seemed they were all going to the jetty to wave goodbye, no time to himself yet.

As the ferry disappeared, the children and their grandparents waved goodbye; the sun began to sink lower turning the sky a golden red promising some fine weather the next day. Charlie hoped that the next few weeks weren't going to be too boring. Little did he know just what was in store for him.

Chapter 3

The ferry approached its jetty with practised ease. Hetty was fascinated. "Isn't it going a bit fast Dad?"

"No, I think they've done this so many times that they've got it inch perfect Hetty," said Dad

The ferry turned at the last minute and slipped alongside the jetty; a young lad jumped off and tied it up at the front and the back. The ferry had arrived with just three people on board: the driver, the young lad who tied it up and a lady with an empty shopping trolley.

"See you in a couple of hours Sam, I hope it's not too busy at the supermarket," the lady said.

"The ferries will be running at 20 past and 10 to the hour this afternoon Jean. See you later," said Sam as he handed her shopping trolley to her.

Hetty stood in the small queue waiting to get on board, watching what was going on all around her. Sam was dressed in surfer shorts with a scruffy T-shirt, flip-flops and had a mop of straggly hair; Hetty decided right away that he looked nice and friendly.

"Mind your step, we'll sort your tickets out on board to save time," said Sam.

"On you go Hetty, find us a seat," said Dad.

Hetty jumped onto the small ferry and settled down with her back to the jetty, looking across the small stretch of rough water between them and the end of the sand spit where the beach huts stood.

"Well, this is a real adventure, isn't it Hetty? I feel like we are going abroad. Have you remembered your passport?" joked Dad.

Hetty could feel the excitement growing in her tummy. The ferry was on its way and Hetty could hardly contain herself.

"Whoa, what's that?' she shrieked, jumping up out of her seat. "There's something under my seat hitting me on the legs!"

"Let's have a look it's probably a loose rope or something," said Dad.

They peered under the seat and saw two black eyes staring back at them.

"I expect that's Bob, let's have a look," said Sam. "Come on boy, out you come. He often stows away, I think he likes the ride."

And right on cue, a small brown and white scruffy dog strolled out from under the seat, looking very pleased with himself.

"That's the third time this week he's joined us for the ride," said Sam.

The small dog walked down the ferry, between the seats; he seemed to be checking all was well before coming back and settling down at Hetty's feet.

"He thinks he's part of the crew," said Sam.

Hetty sat down on the floor next to Bob so that she could stroke him. "He's lovely, who does he belong to?"

"A lady called Grace owns him but he is a bit of a free spirit. A bit like Grace I suppose. They live in their beach hut during the summer. Are you on a day trip?"

"We are staying for the summer as well," said Hetty proudly as she continued to stroke Bob, who seemed quite content with the attention.

"Hold on Hetty, we need to make sure the hut is OK first," said Dad, but Hetty just knew it would be.

Looking out over the ferry rails Hetty could see the line of brightly coloured beach huts stretched along the sand spit and between the huts she caught glimpses of the beach and open sea on the far side. There were a few people walking along the spit towards a large building that looked like a café near the end of the line of huts. The ferry started to turn in towards a wooden jetty that reached out into the water.

"Here we are then," said Dad as Sam tied the ferry up. "Now we just need to find number 65 and hope that the key still works."

Sam and the ferryman helped the passengers off.

"Where's Bob? He was here a moment ago, but he seems to have disappeared, do you think he's OK?" asked a worried Hetty

Sam laughed and pointed to the beach.

"He was the first one off. Look, he's already heading home." They looked at the beach and could see the small dog trotting happily along the water's edge.

Hetty and her dad walked down the jetty and stood on the beach silently, taking in the scene in front of them.

"Come on Hetty!" Dad headed off in search of the hut.

Hetty stood rooted to the spot for a moment; her sense of excitement had been replaced by a feeling of utter joy and happiness. She saw before her what she could only describe as a magical place. Small boats bobbed about in the bay, seagulls called happily to each other, small children played by the water's edge watched by their parents. The huts close by looked beautiful; she hoped theirs would be as lovely.

"HETTY!" called Dad.

She headed off down the beach after Dad with a huge smile on her face.

"From what I remember the hut is around here somewhere, quite close to the shower block over there. This one is number 71 and we want number 65," said Dad. They walked on down the line, on the harbour side of the huts. Every hut was different, some had little verandas in front of them, some looked like they were on stilts with kayaks and sail boards packed underneath them, there were tables and chairs in front, lots of barbecues, some huts were really big and new, others quite small and a little tatty.

"Here we are," said Dad. He was standing outside a hut that looked very unloved, it must have been a smart dark blue colour many years ago but now it looked very shabby.

Hetty and her Dad stood in front of the hut taking it all in. The look on their faces was very different. Dad looked defeated but Hetty was smiling from ear to ear.

"Come on Dad, let's see what's inside."

It took a few minutes to get the lock open but once inside they found themselves in quite a large room that had a seating area, a small kitchen and bunk beds. In the corner there was a stepladder that disappeared up into the roof.

It was all very dirty and dark and even Hetty was a little disappointed by the condition of the inside. Cobwebs hung from every corner, it smelt damp and a film of dust and grime covered every surface. The sea air had covered the windows with salt and sand so that it was impossible to see out.

"I'm not sure this is going to work Hetty," said Dad.

Before Hetty had a chance to try and convince her dad that this was going to be fine, there was a knock on the door and a lady's voice called out.

"Hello! Is anyone there?"

"Hi, yes." Dad and Hetty turned to see who was calling.

"I'm Sophie, we own the hut next door and this is my little boy, Jack."

She was standing in the doorway holding the hand of a very young boy who was holding a bucket and spade that was nearly as big as he was.

"Oh hi, I'm Mike and this is my daughter Hetty; we have come over to see what state my parents' hut is in. We had hoped to stay for the summer but as you can see that's probably not going to be possible. It's such a mess!" said Dad as he looked anxiously around the inside of the hut.

"But Dad this can all be cleaned up really easily, it doesn't matter what the outside looks like and we can sort this out. Please Dad, it will be brilliant to stay here and you are always telling me that nothing worth doing is ever easy."

Hetty was desperate for Dad to agree.

"You would be amazed how quickly you can turn these huts around with a bit of effort," said Sophie.

Hetty shot Sophie a smile and Sophie winked back. Hetty really liked her already; she seemed to be on Hetty's side and could see how important it was to her.

"Why don't you pop into us next door for a cup of tea whilst you think about it?"

"That's very kind of you; yes that would be great, we'll be round in a few minutes," said Dad, who still didn't looked convinced about the hut.

"Look at it Hetty. I know you want to stay here but just look at it."

"This really won't take very long to clean up Dad, I promise I will help. Please Dad," begged Hetty.

"Let's go next door and have that cup of tea and think about it."

When they got next door Hetty was amazed at the stark contrast between their run-down hut and Sophie and her husband Nigel's beautiful hut. The outside was freshly painted a light sea-blue. Inside, everything was clean and tidy, the cushions and curtains were all covered in jolly blue and red stripes. Hetty thought it was lovely and that the whole hut felt very homely. She thought it was going to persuade Dad that this was a really bad idea but to her surprise she heard Dad and Nigel talking about what could be done with their hut. Nigel was telling Dad that their hut had been in a worse state than number 65 when they had first bought it. Nigel proudly showed Dad a before and after photo that they had in a frame on the wall.

"Wow!" exclaimed Dad. "You wouldn't know it was the same hut. Did it take you very long?"

Nigel started to explain to Dad what they had done to transform their hut into its present condition.

Hetty felt like she was holding her breath waiting for his decision. The more he spoke to Nigel the more confident Hetty felt that she would be staying for the summer.

"Don't worry Hetty, I'm sure everything will be fine," said Sophie. "Let's leave them to it. Come on outside with Jack and me. He loves to build sandcastles but he could do with some help."

They left the men inside and Hetty spent the next half an hour helping Sophie's two-year-old, Jack, build sandcastles. She had forgotten what fun that was. No sooner had she built the sandcastles, Jack would take great delight in jumping on them, laughing loudly as they fell apart.

Finally Dad came out with Nigel and Sophie, who had nipped inside to see how they were getting on.

"Right Hetty, this is what I think we should do. Let's have a go and see what it's like when we've cleaned it up. Sophie and Nigel have agreed to keep an eye on you and lend you some cleaning materials so that you can start the big clean-up, while I go back and pick up the sleeping bags, clothes, food and bits that we will need for the next few days. OK?"

Hetty ran up and threw her arms around him. She couldn't speak: at that moment she felt like the luckiest girl in the world.

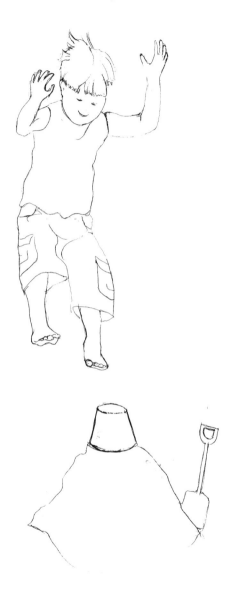

Chapter 4

"Well, where do I start?"

Hetty stood in the middle of the hut looking at the mess and dirt that surrounded her. Standing there, she felt a kind of sadness; it was as if the hut was miserable about its dilapidated state.

"Don't worry hut, Hetty is here to make you better."

And off she went, scrubbing the floors, washing the windows and clearing out all the old rubbish. Spiders scuttled out of the way trying to find a safe corner to hide in. Along the way she found four old buckets, two broken spades, a set of saucepans, a colourful kite with badly knotted string and a dog's bone.

By late afternoon Hetty was exhausted. The beach hut looked much better than it had when she had started that morning; it was almost unrecognisable. As was Hetty, who looked like she had rolled around in the dust and muck! She looked in the newly cleaned mirror; the face that looked back at her had black smudges all over it and she could see a halo of cobwebs clinging to her blonde curls. What a sight! She hoped Dad would remember her shower gel.

"That's it, I've had it. How does that feel, hut?"

Hetty stood there almost waiting for a reply. The whole feel of the hut had changed in those few hours, it looked bright and fresh and perhaps a little cosy and welcoming, almost like next door. Sophie had popped in a couple of times during the afternoon to see how she was getting on and couldn't believe what a transformation Hetty had made. Hetty hugged herself with pleasure.

Looking around she felt quite proud of her efforts but she could also see that there was still a lot to do.

"At least we won't be attacked by giant spiders tonight," she thought as she remembered the number of cobwebs and spiders that had appeared throughout the day.

Outside, the light was already starting to fade; Hetty stood on the hut's decking taking in the scene laid out in front of her. As she watched the last of the day trippers heading home on the ferry she could feel an excitement bubbling up in her. She had never actually stayed overnight at the beach hut before and a sense of great adventure was starting to grow inside her.

"This is going to be great."

"Eh, you talking to me?" said a boy's voice.

Hetty hadn't realised she had spoken out loud and was now really confused because the voice appeared to come from nowhere.

"Is anybody there?" asked Hetty.

At that moment a streak of brown and white flew past the hut and disappeared under the hut next door.

"Come here you pesky animal," said the voice again.

charlie

Around the corner came a large boy in a red T-shirt with a stick in his hand. He didn't sound very friendly; Hetty tried to back up into the shadows of the hut. Something told Hetty that this was not a friendly local. From her vantage point she watched the boy as he came closer to the hut. Something seemed very familiar about him. Hetty had the feeling that she had seen this boy before. Just at that moment Hetty caught her foot on the veranda of the hut. The boy turned around in Hetty's direction.

Oh no, Hetty knew that face. It was Charlie Parsons, school bully from the year above her at their junior school, and all-round nasty person. Luckily Charlie seemed more interested in chasing whatever it was that was now hiding underneath the next-door hut. Hetty watched as Charlie puffed past and got down on all fours to peer under the hut shouting, "Hey Mutt, give me back my hot dog or I'll make you into a hot dog!"

Charlie was getting very frustrated.

"Oh come on dog, that's my dinner you are eating. Where have you gone?"

Very quietly Hetty opened the door of her hut and slipped inside, deciding it was wise to stay inside until the coast was clear but something caught her eye as she moved to the back of the hut. Out of the back window she saw the small terrier disappearing between the huts on the other side by the main beach. Bob didn't seem to be in any hurry, trotting along quite happily with a huge hot dog in his mouth.

Hetty smiled to herself as she could hear Charlie shouting all sorts of threats to Bob who he thought was still underneath the next-door hut. Eventually the shouting stopped and Hetty felt it was OK to nip out, but just to be on the safe side she went out through the door at the back of the hut.

Sophie was outside the back of the huts using the shelter that this provided to light a BBQ.

"I've finished clearing up and was just going to have a quick look around if that's OK," explained Hetty.

"Fine by me, but don't be too long as it will be getting dark soon," said Sophie.

"OK, I've got my phone on me."

Just as she said that her phone rang; it was Dad.

"Hi Hetty, the reception isn't very good so I will keep it quick. I've got so much stuff that I can't manage it all on the ferry. There's a Land Rover that the beach hut owners can use and I've booked it for half an hour's time. I've got some food as well. Could you meet me in half an hour to help me unload?"

"Will do, Dad."

"Hetty...? Hetty...? Oh, this is useless!" And then the phone went dead.

Just enough time, she thought, to have a look about. Hetty headed off towards the end of the spit. The lines of beach huts took on a different look in the early evening light. Quite a few were occupied; some already had their curtains drawn and the lights on. They looked really cosy. Other huts had groups of people barbequing happily outside on the sand. The smell of sausages and burgers cooking was delicious. Hetty realised she was really hungry.

During the day there were always people coming and going to and from the ferry, some headed to the beach carrying picnics, towels, surfboards and buckets and spades, walkers made for the headland armed with hiking boots, backpacks and dogs to explore the various marked walks.

At this time of the day the whole place seemed to settle down, almost as though it was taking a deep relaxing breath and was looking forward to the quietening evening and the peaceful night ahead. You could almost feel nature taking over as the visitors all went home.

Hetty felt very lucky to be allowed to stay in this special place and she made a pact with herself to enjoy every minute of it - the people, place, and the adventures she was sure she would have.

Walking down past the Beach House Restaurant she could see a few people having an early supper. More food! Hetty's stomach started to growl. I hope Dad's bought something good for supper.

Just ahead she could see a large boy picking up stones and skimming them on the water. Hetty got a little closer and fully intended to have a quick chat and to join in when she recognised the red T-shirt from earlier in the evening. It was Charlie. Hetty changed direction quickly and headed to the main beach side of the huts. Looking back, as she made her escape, she presumed Charlie wasn't skimming stones but was trying to hit the small boats that were moored just off-shore. Typical, he hadn't changed.

Doubling back on herself, Hetty was back at her hut in no time. She felt a little disappointed that her exploration had been cut short but she had the whole of the holiday ahead of her.

When she arrived back, Dad was already there unloading a lot of boxes and bags from the back of the Land Rover with an elderly man.

"Hi," said the man.

"This is Steve, Hetty. Thanks for your help Steve, your Land Rover service is really useful as we are not allowed to bring cars up here. I don't know how I would have managed without it."

"No problem, you've got my number if you need me again," said Steve as he waved good-bye.

"Come on Hetty, let's get this lot inside."

Dad found the camping light he had brought with him and placed it on the table. As he turned it on and looked around he exclaimed: "Wow, what a difference you have made to this old hut, Hetty!"

"Thanks.," Hetty looked around her with a sense of pride. Yeah, she had made a big difference.

"I hope you are hungry. I've bought a massive pizza," said Dad.

"I'm absolutely starving; all this cleaning has made me really hungry."

Hetty sat at the rickety old wooden table that she covered with a bright striped tablecloth that Dad had brought with him.

"Here we are then," said Dad as he sat down and opened the biggest pizza box Hetty had ever seen. Maybe it was because she was so hungry but Hetty thought it was the most delicious pizza she had ever tasted, especially as she was never allowed takeaways when Mum was around.

Dad had a beer and Hetty had a coke.

"Let's raise a glass to our new summer house, Hetty's Hut," said Dad.

As they clinked their glasses together, Hetty and Dad sat in companionable silence; both had smiles on their faces.

"I think this is going to be great fun," Dad winked at Hetty. "I told you it would work out OK."

It didn't take them long to polish off their supper.

Parp, parp.

"Did you hear something?" asked Hetty.

"Like what?" asked Dad.

Parp, parp. There it was again.

Hetty got up to see where the noise was coming from. As she went out of the hut she heard someone say, "Hello Hetty."

Hetty was confused, as in front of her was quite a sight. An elderly lady was perched on an adult trike dressed in very unusual multicoloured, mismatched clothes. The trike had a small box attached to the back, full of bits and pieces that Hetty presumed this lady had found on the beach.

Parp, parp.

"Do you like my new hooters? I found them underneath one of the empty huts," said the lady.

"Do I know you?" asked Hetty

"Ohhh, you don't remember me. Well, that doesn't happen very often. They do say once you've met me you never… I'm Grace and I live next door with Bob my dog," said Grace.

A glimmer of a memory came to Hetty. "Did I go sailing with you when I was very small?" she asked.

Grace clapped her hands and said, "You do remember, yes we spent some time together with your nana a few summers ago."

The bits and pieces in Grace's bike basket caught Hetty's eye. "What have you got in your box, Grace?" asked Hetty politely.

"Just some old ropes, a small rope cage that looks like a miniature lobster pot and... Did you know that the fish were running today, I heard that from old... Have you seen Bob anywhere?"

Hetty couldn't quite work out what Grace was talking about, as she seemed to have a habit of not finishing one sentence before starting the next. She was so different to

Hetty's own Gran. They must be about the same age but Hetty thought that that was their only similarity.

Gran was soft and loving but everything about her seemed quite pale in comparison to Grace. Her clothes were conventional, her manners perfect and her whole appearance was as a grandmother's should be.

Grace, however, wore rainbow-coloured clothes that didn't match and, as far as Hetty knew, her only footwear was a pair of bright yellow crocs that had paint splattered all over them. Her hair was a wiry nest of greyness.

When Grace spoke she seemed to lose control of her false teeth which Hetty thought might be why she never seemed to finish a sentence.

At that moment Grace must have remembered that she needed to be somewhere else.

"BOTHER AND BLAST!" she shouted and then laughed really loudly as if she knew it was wrong to use that type of language but that she had decided that, at her age, she could do what she liked and didn't much care what the world thought of her. And, oh, that laugh! Hetty was sure nobody would ever describe it as a gentle female giggle. It was more like a huge guffaw. Grace was larger than life in every sense of the phrase. Hetty knew she was going to love Grace and her eccentric ways.

"I saw a dog that might have been Bob about an hour ago. He was heading towards the woods," said Hetty, deliberately leaving out the part about the hot dog, in case it got Bob into trouble.

"Oh poo," said Grace before starting to peddle quickly in the direction Hetty had pointed. "He's in trouble with those Londoners again for digging holes in their garden."

She shouted over her shoulder, "I keep telling them he's a dog and that's what he is supposed to do. See you later. Oh and I must tell you about the..."

And that was that. Like a human, rainbow-coloured whirlwind, Grace was off again.

No sooner had Grace peddled away than the small brown and white dog came trotting around the corner.

"Bob, where have you been? Grace is looking for you."

It seemed to Hetty that Bob spent most of his time either exploring the area, taking secret trips on the ferry, stealing food or fast asleep under Grace's beach hut.

"What have you got there Bob?" asked Hetty as Bob deposited a large key at her feet. Bob sat there expectantly waiting to be congratulated on his find.

Sitting down next to him she picked up the key. "You are a good boy Bob." Bob wagged his tail and looked very pleased with himself.

Hetty was sure that Bob understood every word she said to him. In fact she believed that he was part of some great big secret pact between all dogs. She was convinced that they could all speak as humans do but that they had agreed not to let anyone know about this skill. Anyway, this was her theory but she kept it to herself. She had once decided to see if anyone else thought the same and shared her idea with Amy at school. Amy had laughed and had spread it around the school. For the next month, everyone had barked words at Hetty and she realised that telling anyone had been a huge mistake. She decided not to share her ideas about dogs with anyone in future. Bob, however, sat and listened to her, moving his head from side to side in an intelligent way and he didn't make fun of her.

The key Bob had found was bigger than any Hetty had seen before. It was rusty in places but was still solid and heavy. It had a strange pattern on the top and intricate design along the shaft. She wondered what size lock it would fit.

"Where did you find this Bob?" Bob just sat there wagging his tail and then trotted off to the next-door hut where he promptly curled up on the porch.

"What was the noise?" asked Dad when Hetty went back inside.

"It was the lady from the next-door hut, Grace; she was looking for her dog Bob, you know, the dog from the ferry. She's gone off looking for him and he has come back and is now fast asleep on their porch. He brought this key with him. He must have found it somewhere. Shall I put it in the drawer in the kitchen to keep it safe in case someone has lost it?"

"That's a good idea. I remember Grace, she took you sailing with her when you were little," said Dad.

"You really enjoyed it, perhaps you could go again this summer but for now I think we need to get some sleep. You've done a great job with the hut today Hetty, but you must be very tired."

All of a sudden she did feel really tired.

"I'm off to bed; see you in the morning Dad. Night, night."

Hetty gave Dad a big hug and climbed the ladder to her little sleeping platform in the roof where she fell fast asleep as soon as her head touched the pillow.

Chapter 5

The next morning Hetty woke up early; the sun was shining through the small window level with her bed. She stretched and smiled to herself as she realised where she was. She wriggled across the platform in her sleeping bag like a caterpillar and peered over the edge to see if Dad was awake in the bottom bunk. Hetty could see him with his head under the pillow and could tell that he was still asleep. It was very early but Hetty was impatient to go out and explore. Carefully, so as not to wake Dad, she pulled on a pair of shorts and a T-shirt and, as quietly as possible, climbed down the ladder and crept out of the door, closing it silently behind her. Standing on the veranda in the early morning sunshine she looked around her. The harbour was beautiful and still. Hetty could hear the gentle sound of the waves from the beach side of the sand spit. A fishing boat was coming back into the harbour followed by some noisy gulls, all hoping to pick up any fish bits that were dropped over the side.

Hetty decided to go for a walk; she found herself retracing her route from the day before. There weren't many people about, a few early dog walkers and the owners of the Beach House Restaurant and Café who were opening the shutters and putting the chairs out ready for breakfast; apart from them no one else seemed to be around.

As she walked on, she could see that the line of huts was coming to an end and soon she found herself on a wide pathway with a densely wooded area ahead of her. She wasn't sure which way to go; if she turned left she could see that she would have to climb the hill to the top of the headland, if she turned to the right she would be able to follow the path alongside the woods. Just at that moment Bob appeared on the track heading right.

"Which way is best Bob?"

Bob set off to the right; after a few metres he stopped, looked back at Hetty expectantly with his head on one side and barked.

"Ah, you want me to go that way do you? OK, Bob you lead the way." She set off after him with the woods on her left and the harbour on her right, wandering along, admiring the wild flowers and watching the rabbits scurrying away into the undergrowth as they heard her coming.

After a short distance, she noticed that the path was fenced on one side. A fairly big shed was set a little way back from the path. Hetty decided to have a rest and, leaning on the fence gazing into the woods, wondered what other animals lived in the undergrowth.

BUMP!

"Aaghh. Ssshhhhh."

Hetty looked around to see where the noise had come from. No one behind her, no one in front. She frowned; the noise sounded as though it had come from the shed. Bob seemed to have completely disappeared. Should she investigate where the noise was coming from or ignore it? What if it was a wild animal or a strange person? What wild animals could it be? Foxes and badgers possibly? No, it sounded more human than that. Well, there was only one way to find out. Hetty looked at the shed from the other side of the fence; it had a big sign nailed to it saying 'KEEP OUT. PRIVATE PROPERTY'. She decided to climb over the fence and hide behind a tree to keep watch. Then came another muffled sound and a thud. Hetty decided to go to investigate. Quietly creeping towards the shed she wondered what she would find. An animal...? A person...? What else it might be? There it was again... The sound of movement. If it was a person then they must be alive. Maybe it was an animal trapped in the hut, she bravely walked up to the door and pushed it, it didn't move - obviously locked tight.

Hetty walked around the side furthest away from the path and saw a window; it was quite high up but looked as though it was unlocked. She needed something to stand on to be able to see inside. Looking around, Hetty saw a tree stump a few feet away, she dragged it over and, taking care not to get up too quickly, she climbed up and peered through the grimy window. She couldn't see much so she cupped her hands around her eyes to stop the sun reflecting off the glass. As her eyes got used to the dark she could see some machinery and old sacks on the floor. She tried the window; it wasn't locked but it opened outwards so she carefully shifted herself back a bit and ducked her head down so that she could pull it open. She popped her head up inside and looked around the gloomy interior; out of the corner of her eye something moved at the back of the hut. Hetty jumped back almost falling off the tree stump. Steadying herself, she looked again as Bob appeared from behind an old wheelbarrow in the corner of the shed.

"Oh Bob. How did you get in there? Can't you get out?"

No answer, so the only thing to do was to climb in and rescue him. Propping the window open with a stick Hetty hauled herself up so that she was balanced on the window edge, she got her leg over the ledge and manoeuvred herself so that she was sitting astride the window, then she lifted the other leg over and dropped down into the hut. It smelt dusty and old. Standing still, Hetty listened. Bob seemed to have disappeared.

"Where are you? Come here you silly dog."

It was very dark in the shed and Hetty began to feel scared. She could hear her own heart pounding in her ears but she could also hear breathing and she was sure that it came from the other side of the shed, it didn't sound like Bob.

"Oh help! What on earth is it? I could be trapped in here with a wild animal." Beads of sweat were breaking out on her forehead. She shivered with fear. Moving as carefully as she could she crept to the back of the shed and then jumped out of her skin as a figure stepped out in front of her. The light from the window caught the figure's face and Hetty could see that it was a boy. He was looking really scared and trying to hide something or someone behind him.

Oh my goodness! Hetty couldn't believe her eyes. She didn't know what she'd expected or what she was going to do. She stood still staring at the boy who stared back at her. He looked as frightened as she felt but not dangerous.

Plucking up all her courage she cleared her throat and managed to say, "Hhhhhhhhhello, I'm Hetty."

She paused not really knowing what else to say. "Who are you?" she asked.

The boy still looked frightened and didn't answer her.

"Um... I'm not going, not going to hurt you." Hetty didn't quite know what to do so she tried again.

"What's your name?"

Still no response, it suddenly occurred to her that the boy didn't understand her and looking at him more closely she realised that he didn't look like an English boy and his clothes were a little odd and not very clean. He was about her age, a bit taller than her with dark hair and skin, not black exactly, not white either. Hetty decided to try again; she thought about it for a few minutes.

"OK." She pointed at herself and smiled, "Hetty" she said and pointed at the boy "You?"

The boy looked at her and smiled back. "Hasan." he said pointing at his chest and moving to one side he revealed what he'd been hiding, a small girl crouched in the corner, her big brown eyes and dark curly hair looking from Hasan to Hetty, fearfully. She looked a lot younger than Hetty. He pointed to her and said, "Kaya."

Hetty was delighted that her communication had worked but what now? Whoever could these children be? They looked like they could be brother and sister. Whatever were they doing here in this dark, gloomy shed? They were clearly frightened about something. Hetty was unsure what to do.

Suddenly there was a snuffling noise and through a small gap in the wall behind Kaya Bob appeared wagging his tail and looking pleased with himself.

Hasan and Kaya had obviously met Bob before and they patted him and smiled.

It occurred to Hetty that the children might be hungry; she was certainly ready for breakfast. She tried her miming again and, pointing to her mouth, she made eating signs, rubbed her tummy and then pointed to them with a questioning look. They looked at her and nodded their heads vigorously.

"OK, I'll be back." Hetty stuck her thumbs up. "OK?"

They nodded again and Hetty looked for something to climb on, Hasan showed her how to get out using the old wheelbarrow in the corner. Hetty smiled and waved to them as she dropped to the ground, she called to Bob and ran back to Dad just in time for breakfast.

Dad looked up as Hetty ran up the steps to the hut panting. "Hey Hetts, where have you been? You sound like you've run a marathon. Who's chasing you?"

"No one," Hetty gasped "I thought I might be…" she took a big breath, "…late."

Dad smiled. "Here, I've done cheese sandwiches for breakfast. Are you hungry?"

"Mmm, great. I'm starving." Hetty reached out for the sandwich. "Thanks." She opened her mouth to take a big bite and then stopped as she thought about the two children she'd just left in the dark little shed.

She closed her mouth and swallowed. "Um… Could I have a drink please Dad?"

Dad got up and went to the back of the hut. "Cup of tea or juice?"

Hetty thought for a second. "A cup of tea please." She thought that this would distract Dad for long enough for her to hide the cheese sandwich so that she could then take it back to the shed. Sure enough as Dad waited for the kettle to boil Hetty had enough time to hide the sandwich in her backpack and sit back down, licking her lips as though she'd eaten it herself.

"Crumbs, you were hungry. Do you want another one?" Dad asked as he sat back down with the teapot and two mugs.

"I can make it Dad, you eat yours." Hetty got up and went into the little kitchen; she got out the loaf and cheese.

"Do you want another one Dad?"

"No thanks, love. I'm fine."

All she had to do now was escape again with the first sandwich, get some water and get back to Hasan and Kaya as soon as possible. Hetty made the new sandwich and took it over to join Dad who was pouring himself another mug of tea.

"Well, guess what I've got planned for today, Hetty."

Oh no! He has a plan. Her stomach sank; it had never occurred to her that Dad might have something organised for today.

"Um, no idea Dad, tell me."

"Well I bumped in to Grace last night at the shower block and she has agreed to take you sailing today; isn't that kind of her? You really enjoyed it when you were younger and as you worked so hard yesterday we thought it would be a lovely treat for you."

Dad looked so pleased with himself that Hetty really couldn't say anything else except, "Oh that's really great Dad, thanks. when are we going?"

Hetty's mind was racing. What about the children they really needed some food, they looked so hungry and they must be thirsty as well.

"More or less straight away, I said I'd take you to meet her as soon as we'd had breakfast."

Hetty's heart sank.

Chapter 6

Sailing! Dad had organised for Grace to take her sailing. Now normally, Hetty would have really enjoyed this sort of thing but she was so focused on getting the food and drink to the children that she really didn't feel able to enjoy anything.

"Grace is a really good sailor and she has a little dinghy moored up on the beach which she is going to take you out in and teach you how to sail. Isn't that great?" Dad was full of enthusiasm.

"Thanks Dad, I'm sure it will be fun," said Hetty, trying to sound more excited than she really was.

"Look, there's Grace down by her dinghy. Off you go; you deserve this treat after all your hard work yesterday."

Hetty headed down to the beach waving to Sam on the ferryboat as she went. She quickly spotted Grace getting the dinghy ready. Bob was having great fun, launching himself again and again into the shallows next to the dinghy.

"Hi there Hetty, ignore Bob, I think he's chasing fish. Probably thinks... Boat's all ready to go, pop this lifejacket on and we can be off," said Grace in her usual confused way.

Hetty did as she was asked; she then stepped gingerly into the boat as Grace pushed it off from the beach.

"Wooooooaaaa! It's really wobbly on the water, Grace."

"You'll soon get used to it. Sit still or you will tip us over," said Grace as she clambered into the little dinghy and started to pull at different ropes.

"Oh, forgot to ask, can you swim?"

"Yes, I've got my 1,000 metre certificate," replied Hetty proudly.

"Look, Bob wants to come with us!" Hetty pointed into the water at the little dog who was swimming as fast as he could after the dinghy.

"Come on you," said Grace as she grabbed Bob by the scruff of his neck and plopped him into the bottom of the dinghy.

Bob shook himself and covered Hetty in cold salt water.

"Thanks Bob," laughed Hetty.

"Right, where shall we go? I know. We'll head... and after that we could..." muttered Grace.

Hetty decided that she would know where they were going once they got there.

* * *

Charlie had arrived at the beach as the dinghy was just leaving. He saw Grace climb in and had just spotted that pesky dog who had stolen his hot dog yesterday evening. The dog saw him and swam off after the dinghy.

"I'll catch up with you soon," muttered Charlie to himself. Charlie strained his eyes to see who else was in the boat. There was a girl in the boat with big bushy blonde hair. She looked familiar, just like a girl he had known at junior school. What was her name? No it couldn't be, it's probably someone who looks like her but that hair was unforgettable, he always wondered how she combed it. Surely no one else could have such a wild mop of blonde curls. He remembered teasing her about it. "What was her name? Harriet? Henrietta? H… H…" He was sure it started with an H. "Hetty! That's it, Hetty Webster."

"What on earth was she doing here? I thought she had moved away."

Charlie stood for a while shielding his eyes from the sun watching the dinghy sail away. When he turned away to look along the line of the beach huts. He noticed a man dressed in dark clothes standing outside a strange-looking black hut that he hadn't really noticed before.

"That's odd." Charlie watched the man for a few minutes. He's watching the dinghy with Grace, Hetty and Bob in it.

"What's he looking at? I wonder why he's so interested in them." Charlie wondered out loud. Just at that moment the man turned around to stare in the direction of Charlie, almost as if he knew that he was being watched. The man looked strange. A shiver ran up Charlie's spine and he looked away as quickly as he could.

The dinghy was now a long way away, heading up the river towards Christchurch. Charlie could just make out its blue sails in the distance.

When he looked back the man had disappeared. Charlie was bored and decided to go to investigate.

The hut that the man had been standing outside looked completely different to the others on the spit. They were all lovely bright and pastel colours but this hut was sinister looking. It was larger and painted black, even the windows were black.

There was no sign of the man and so Charlie climbed onto a rock to try to look into one of the windows. He couldn't see very much but then he noticed a crack in the next windowpane. Either side of the crack was a piece of glass that you could just about see through. Charlie looked through and could see into part of the hut. It didn't seem to have any furniture in it but was cluttered with ropes, lobster pots and some electrical bits and pieces. There seemed to be an old blanket in the corner.

"Oi! What you think you doing?"

Charlie felt a strong hand grip his shoulder and pull him off the rock.

"You nosey boy, it rude to spy on people." The man had a strange accent. Charlie could feel his heart almost beating out of his chest. He was spun around and found himself looking up into the face of the man he'd been watching earlier. The stranger's dark hooded eyes stared down at him menacingly. He had black hair, beard and moustache. He didn't look very friendly and certainly wasn't local. Charlie had never seen him around before.

Charlie didn't want to look at him so stared straight in front at the man's dirty navy blue sweatshirt.

"What you say?" the man's voice was a growl.

Charlie tried to think of an excuse for being there but he was so frightened he couldn't think straight.

"You speak to me," the man ordered

"I... I was." Charlie stammered

"Yes, what?" the man demanded whilst still holding his collar.

Charlie thought frantically, what could he say?

"I... I was looking for my dog," he said, relieved to have thought of something "He's a small brown and white dog and has a scarf around his neck."

"Oh that dog, he gone in boat, you keep away from my hut. Understand?"

"Yes, yes, sorry. I understand," spluttered Charlie as the navy blue man let go of him.

Charlie wanted to get away from there as quickly as he could but the man had another question.

"Have you seen two kids, one boy, one girl?"

"No... no... but if I do I'll let you know."

Charlie started to go.

"You make sure you tell me, now go away," he said in his faltering English. The foreign accent seemed to make him sound even more menacing.

Charlie didn't need to be told twice, he shot off down the beach as fast as he could. He was in such a hurry that he didn't notice that Grace and Hetty were back from their sail and were heading up the beach.

"That was really great, thank you Grace. I'm sorry we had to cut it short but I think I ate too much pizza last night which made me feel a little sick."

"Never mind, we can go again anytime. Let me know when you are feeling better."

Grace walked off, calling out for Bob who had disappeared again.

Hetty felt bad about telling a white lie as she was actually feeling fine but she had to find some way of getting back early so that she could take food to the two children. They must be so hungry.

"Ouch! Watch where you're going!" cried out Hetty as she collided head on with Charlie who was so intent on getting away from the navy blue man that he wasn't looking where he was going.

"Sorry Hetty," said Charlie.

"Oh, you know my name." Hetty was astonished that he would remember her. After all, she was a whole year younger than him.

"I remember you and your hair from primary school." Charlie laughed.

Hetty pushed her unruly curls away from her face and felt her cheeks get warm.

"What's the hurry anyway?" she asked.

"There's a strange man over there, who's been watching you out sailing. I tried to see into his hut but he caught me, he's not from around here and he's a bit scary."

It surprised Hetty to hear Charlie admit to being scared; she thought he was not scared of anyone. This man must be frightening.

"I think we should steer clear of him," but it was his next comment that made Hetty gasp. "He wanted to know if I had seen two children, a boy and a girl., I have to tell him if I see them, I don't know why he's so interested in them. I wouldn't like to be in their shoes when he catches them. He gives me the creeps."

Hetty started to feel a sense of dread. This was too much of a coincidence. She needed to know more.

"Why does he give you the creeps?" she asked.

"Well, he's really big and strong. He grabbed my collar, spun me around and when he spoke to me, he was really nasty."

As they walked back towards the huts together, Charlie said, "Just so you know what he looks like, so you can avoid him, he speaks with a foreign accent and has a big black beard. His navy blue sweatshirt was rank and he smelt awful."

"Which is his hut?" Hetty needed to know so that she could avoid him as much as possible.

Charlie pointed to the black hut, "That's the one; it looks scary just like its owner."

When they got back to the line of friendly huts, Hetty and Charlie said goodbye, Hetty with another problem to worry about and Charlie still shaken from his encounter with the foreigner.

Chapter 7

As soon as Hetty got back she turned her mind to the problem of getting food to the children, she was sure they would be wondering what had happened to her. She hoped they didn't think that she had deserted them.

The hut was quiet and locked, where was Dad? She tried to remember what he had said. Was he going anywhere? she didn't think so. They had agreed that the key would be hidden under a rock underneath the steps when they went out. She jumped down, retrieved it and opened up the hut. As she went in she saw a piece of paper on the table with Dad's writing on.

Gone to town see you about 5.30pm. Dad. xx

Hetty looked at her watch. Half past one, good, plenty of time to get to the children and with Dad out she could get some more food to take with her. Quickly, Hetty made herself a sandwich and another couple to take with her; she wrapped them in some foil along with the sandwich from breakfast. She found a bottle of water, some Kit Kats and a couple of apples and carefully packed them all in her back pack. Hetty took an apple for herself and decided to eat it on the way as she really needed to get to Hasan and Kaya as quickly as possible.

Hetty opened the door, locked it behind her and, returning the key to its hiding place, swung the back pack onto her shoulders. She set off as fast as she could to the children's shed. She kept a look out as she went, not wanting to bump into the man who had accosted Charlie that morning. She felt sure that he was lurking around somewhere and, even though it was a warm afternoon, she felt a shiver down her spine.

There were lots of people out enjoying the summer sun, children were whizzing about on bikes, trikes and scooters, mums and dads were strolling about with babies and small children in buggies, dogs were sniffing around in the undergrowth, children were digging in the sand and groups of teenagers were lounging around but Hetty saw none of them as she hurried along towards the shed.

As Hetty reached the fence with the 'KEEP OUT' sign, there were many people walking along the path, family groups, couples walking hand in hand and the little Noddy train trundling along taking passengers to the beach huts. Oh dear, what was she going to do? How could she get over the fence and up to the shed without arousing suspicion and being accused of trespassing?

Hetty decided to sit on the fence and that way if it ever did get quieter then she could quickly jump down and run to the hut. She pulled herself up and swivelled around to perch on the top rung and keep watch. She looked at the time, nearly half past two; she couldn't begin to imagine how hungry the children would be. She wondered when they had last eaten and if she would ever find out where they had come from and why they were hiding? Could it be anything to do with Charlie's bearded navy blue man?

Hetty sat and watched but every time she thought the coast was clear another person or group of laughing, care-free people would come around the corner. It was nearly half past three before a bark alerted her to Bob standing in front of her, wagging his tail, head on one side as if to say, "What are you doing here?"

"Hey Bob," Hetty jumped down and knelt in front of him stroking him, an idea forming in her mind. If she could get Bob to wriggle under the fence and run off then she could pretend that he was her dog and, if anyone was watching her, she would have to go after him to get him back. Hetty looked along the fence; now, where had he got through this morning? Suddenly she saw a small gap and led Bob to it. Bending over, she grabbed his necktie and pulled him over to the gap; he poked his nose through and as if he understood exactly what her plan was he wriggled through and ran towards the shed.

Brilliant! Hetty called on all her acting experience which, to date consisted of playing an angel in the school nativity, when she was in Reception class, and a non-speaking part as a weasel in the school play *Wind in the Willows*.

Hetty called out as she jumped off the fence and ran towards the hut, "Bob, Bob! Come back here at once you naughty boy." Bob had completely disappeared but Hetty ran to the window and clambered in the same way as she had done that morning.

She called out softly, "Hasan, Kaya, it's me, Hetty."

As she dropped to the floor she took off her backpack and started to open it. The brother and sister appeared from the shadows, accompanied by Bob.

"Here you are - food and water." Hetty offered the sandwiches, apples and Kit Kats to the children and watched in astonishment as the two starving youngsters crammed the food into their mouths as fast as they possibly could. Just when had they last eaten? She had never seen food disappear so fast, even Ollie couldn't eat that quickly. Bob was sniffing around hoping for some leftovers but there was no chance.

When the children had finished the food they smiled at Hetty and held out their hands, Hetty took their hands and smiled back

"Food OK?" she tried.

They nodded their heads and rubbed their tummies. "OK."

Hetty thought about the words she could teach them.

She nodded her head and said, "Yes" and then shook her head and said, "No". They looked at her and repeated the words with the correct actions. Hetty laughed and clapped. "Good, good." She took the bottle of water and said "Water."

"Yes, water," said Hasan smiling shyly.

Hetty clapped again.

"Yes, water good," Hasan repeated slowly. "Yes, water, good.,"

Hetty suddenly remembered the time. Looking at her watch she saw it was almost four o'clock, she needed to get back before Dad. She took off her watch and showed it to Hameed turning the hands around she said, "Tomorrow."

Hasan looked at her and the watch and then the penny dropped. "Yes, tomorrow," he said.

Hetty was pleased; she tried a bit more "Me, Hetty..." she said, pointing to herself, "...will come tomorrow with more food. OK?"

Hasan and Kaya both nodded and smiled. Hetty wasn't sure they completely understood what she was saying but Hasan was smiling and saying "OK". Hasan said something in his own language and Hetty realised that he must be saying 'thank you'.

So she said "thank you" to him and he tried to repeat the word but the 'th' was hard and it came out as "sank you". Hasan was smiling broadly and Hetty grinned back.

She was worried that they wouldn't stay out of sight; how could she make them understand that they must stay inside the shed?.

"You must stay here." She pointed to the window and shook her head, pointed to them and then to the window again. "No!" she said in a stern voice. "Stay here, OK?"

The children looked at her and then at each other with a puzzled look.

Hetty had an idea. She took Kaya's hand, led her to the window and made to lift her up and encourage her to climb out, then she pulled her back and said, "No, stay here."

The penny dropped and both children nodded at Hetty and she realised with relief that they understood her elaborate play-acting.

"OK, goodbye." Hetty waved to the children, they waved back and helped her to climb out of the window.

Hetty cautiously peered around the corner of the hut, the coast looked clear so she resumed her acting. "Bob! Bob! Where are you?"

Obediently, on cue, Bob entered the stage and trotted over to Hetty.

"Oh you naughty boy, where have you been?" Hetty played to her nonexistent audience. Hurrying back to the fence she climbed over it and dropped down onto the path. Looking left and right she glanced at the time, just right to get back before Dad.

Lost in thought, mulling over the questions she had about the pair of children as she hurried home, she didn't notice the man in the bushes on the left-hand side of the path until she nearly walked into him. He was looking at her intently.

Hetty looked down and tried to walk on but the man stepped into her path and she had to stop. She looked up at the tall, heavily built, bearded man and didn't like what she saw, she was sure he was the same man that had scared Charlie earlier in the day.

"I watching you." The man had a gruff voice and Hetty felt nervous, she stepped back looking over her shoulder hoping to see some people coming along the path but, unlike earlier, there was no one in sight.

Hetty gulped and tried again to step aside but again the man stepped in front of her.

"I ask you questions," he said. "What you doing back there?"

Hetty cleared her throat and pulled herself up to her full height of 4'10".

"I was looking for my friend's dog," she said in as firm a voice as possible; she was sure Grace wouldn't mind. "Why do you want to know?" she asked.

"No ask why, you seen any children here, boy and girl?" The man bent down and peered into her face, she could smell stale cigarettes on his breath; she turned her head away and stepped back again.

"No I haven't seen any strangers, only you." Hetty hoped she sounded braver than she felt. "Who are these children and why do you want them?"

"Too many questions. You to tell me if you see children. You understand me?"

"Well," said Hetty, "I'll be seeing a lot of children, I got here yesterday and there are lots of children here so I really can't help you, sorry."

This time her side-step worked and she started to run as fast as she could back to the beach hut hoping that Dad would be back. After a while she dared to slow down and stole a glance over her shoulder, the man was still standing where she had left him watching her as she ran home.

"Hi Hetty, Hetty!" Charlie was running towards her.

"Are you OK? That's the man who asked me about the children this morning. I saw him talking to you, what was he saying? Was he being nasty to you as well?"

Hetty couldn't ignore him so she stopped and said, "Yes, he was asking me about a girl and a boy, but I haven't seen anyone, have you?" Hetty wasn't going to tell anyone about Hasan and Kaya, she didn't know if she could trust Charlie. She felt responsible for the safety of the frightened children hiding in the shed. She decided to keep quiet but her tummy was churning and she felt really anxious. She realised she needed to move the children to a safer hiding place and quickly.

"I must get back, Dad will be wondering where I am, see you later." Hetty started to walk away.

"Hetty!" Charlie called after her.

She walked on.

"Be careful Hetty, I don't like that man."

"I will, don't worry about me. Might see you tomorrow, Charlie." Hetty hoped she sounded braver than she actually felt. It was nice to feel that he was watching out for her. She started to run to get back before Dad sent out a search party.

Chapter 8

The next day, after a few hours cleaning and tidying their hut it was time for Dad's usual mid-morning cuppa.

"Hetty," called Dad. "Can you nip to the shop and pick up some milk, please?"

"Any chance of an ice cream?"

"Sure."

Outside the hut the day was perfect, a beautiful summer's day, full of the promise of freedom. No school for six whole weeks. Hetty wandered off towards the tiny shop that was attached to The Beach House Restaurant and Café.

She was getting more and more familiar with the huts nearby and their inhabitants. Grace and Bob next door, the Bassetts - Sophie, Nigel and little Jack - the other side and Sam on the ferryboat.

There were a few other huts that were occupied with people that Hetty did not yet know. One of those was the large black hut Charlie had pointed out last night. It lay just past the shop and only had blacked out windows. It was a different shape and size to the rest of the huts. It somehow looked dark and foreboding. As she walked towards the shop she called to Bob to come with her.

In the distance she saw a large man rowing his small rowing boat towards the beach. He threw out his anchor and stepped into the shallow waters. Hetty strained her eyes to see who it was. The man looked huge and was dressed in dark clothes from head to toe, his stride was so big it only took him six steps to reach the line of huts. It was him! It was the creepy man from yesterday.

Hetty turned her back hoping he hadn't seen her. It had looked like the man was heading to the black hut.

"Come on Bob, let's go around the back of the huts and see what he's up to."

She ran up the beach and headed for the huts. As she reached the back of the shop, the man seemed to have vanished. Hetty ran around to the front but he was nowhere to be seen.

"That's odd Bob, he has just disappeared. Weird!"

Hetty went into the shop and bought the milk. Her thoughts turned to the big question – what flavour ice cream to get from the kiosk outside?

'Mint choc chip or strawberry cheesecake flavour? Hmmmm.'

Hetty was so distracted that she walked straight into somebody as she rounded the corner of the shop.

"AAARGH!" said the boy as he fell backwards onto the sand. The force of the collision had also knocked Hetty to the floor.

"Watch where you are going!"

"I'm so sorry, my mind was on ice cream and I didn't see you," said Hetty.

"Oh no," said the boy as the mention of ice cream reminded him of his own cone which was on the floor covered in sand.

"Don't worry," said Hetty. "I will buy you another one. What flavour was it?"

She realised that this would mean that she didn't have enough money for her own ice cream but it was her fault.

"Ryan." said the boy as they got to their feet.

"I'm Hetty."

She liked the look of Ryan, he was about her age, maybe a little older, he was smiling and didn't seem put out about losing his ice cream.

They walked together to the ice cream kiosk. It was attached to the end of the restaurant building, next to the shop and there was a large window that was used as a serving hatch for ice creams.

"What flavour would you like?" Hetty asked.

"Vanilla for me," said Ryan.

"Hey Joe!" shouted Ryan.

A boy who was amongst a group of children waved and headed in their direction followed by the other children.

"Joe, this is Hetty."

Hetty turned around to give Ryan his ice cream.

"Hi, you staying here?"

"Yep, for the whole summer," said Hetty with some pride.

"We'll be seeing a lot of you then as me, Ryan, Megs, Emily and Danni are here till September as well."

As he said each child's name they gave a nod of acknowledgement.

"Megs, check this out," said the girl called Danni.

Danni was pointing at a poster stuck on the kiosk window.

'Midsummer Night's Fancy Dress Party and BBQ at The Beach House.'

"That sounds like fun, but what would we dress up in?" asked Megs.

"We could all go as ghosts or fairies," suggested Hetty.

"Oh great idea! Come on Hetty, let's see what we can find, the party is tomorrow night, so we don't have much time." Megs pulled Hetty by the arm as she tried to wave goodbye to Ryan who was studying his ice cream. Emily and Danni headed off to one of their huts to find more dressing-up supplies.

"We'll meet at Megs in a while," shouted Danni.

"Which hut is yours?" asked Megs.

"I'm on the side that overlooks the harbour, number 65," said Hetty, clutching the milk carton close as they hurried along.

"This is mine," said Megs as they climbed up the decking steps of a beautiful, powder blue beach hut. The hut looked brand new, with a large seating area, a full-size fridge, flat screen TV and cooker.

"WOW! This is amazing!" exclaimed Hetty as she twirled around taking in all the lovely things.

"Come on up," said Megs from somewhere above. Hetty hadn't noticed her disappear upstairs; she climbed the steps in the middle of the hut and found Megs sitting in a large sleeping area. She was rifling through a huge box.

"This is Mum's odds-and-ends box, there's bound to be something in here we can use."

The two girls spent a very happy time searching through the box and trying on all sorts of weird things until Hetty's phone beeped.

"Oh no! I forgot Dad's milk, I need to go."

"OK, I'll catch you later, we usually meet here after supper, if you are free later." said Megs.

"Thanks Megs, hope to see you then."

Hetty headed off as fast as she could towards her hut. Poor Dad he must be gasping for a cup of tea by now.

When Hetty finally arrived at the hut with the milk she was greeted with, "Did you tie the cow back up after you had milked it?"

"Sorry Dad, I met a few of the local kids. They are really nice and friendly, especially Megs and Ryan."

"Well I'm glad you like them. Sophie just popped around from next door and asked if we would mind keeping an eye on Jack for her while she goes shopping this afternoon. Nigel will be there in the hut but he has work to do, so would you mind playing with him for a while so that I can carry on painting the hut?" Dad looked up from his paintwork questioningly.

"No problem Dad, I'll go round after lunch and pick him up, I'm starving. What is there to eat?"

Great, thought Hetty I need to get to Hasan and Kaya; they will be hungry by now and wondering where I am. I'll ask if I can take Jack for a walk and that way I can take him with me to the children in the shed.

Chapter 9

Hetty ate her lunch as fast as she could. Dad looked out to sea, watching the gulls as they wheeled overhead screeching and calling to each other, swooping down low on the lookout for any scraps of food that careless picnickers had left behind.

"You know something Hetty?" Dad was still gazing into the distance.

"What?" Hetty looked over at him.

"I think this could be really fun, this holiday. I'm glad you persuaded me to give it a try. If I can get the hut spruced up quickly then we can just take it easy for the rest of the time, what do you think?"

"Sounds like a plan Dad, I'll clear up the dishes then, so you can get on," said Hetty happily "After that I will go and get Jack from next door. Do you think I'll be allowed to take him for a walk?"

"I would think so, if you don't go too far away and keep your phone switched on. Is it charged? You had better check with Sophie." Dad got up and went down the steps to his paint pot, crouching down to start painting again.

Hetty cleared the remains of the lunch and took the plates into the little kitchen. She needed to get some more food for the children, so hastily packed her rucksack with cheese, bread, apples and some chocolate biscuits, then added a bottle of coke. She zipped it up and shoved it into a cupboard in case Dad came back inside; she then quickly washed up the lunch things, putting them away tidily.

Hetty retrieved her rucksack, jumped down the steps and, making her way across the sand to collect Jack, she knocked at the door.

"Come in Hetty, thank you so much for offering to look after Jack, Nigel is here but he's working so having you to play with will be great, won't it Jack?"

Jack nodded and shyly handed Hetty a train to admire.

"That's OK. It will be fun; I always wanted a younger brother or sister to play with. I've got an older brother but he's really boring. He only likes computer games; he hates going outdoors and loathes the feel of sand."

"Well I'm sure that Jack will love having you to baby-sit, you could take him for a little walk if you like, I'll get his trike for you in case he gets tired, it's got a handle on the back so you can push him if he's slow; it's hard work on the sand but if you stay on the path it's not too bad"

"Great," thought Hetty. "That's perfect."

Sophie went to the back of the hut, and using a metal loop in the floor, opened a trap door. Hetty looked on amazed.

"You've got a cellar as well as an upstairs!" Hetty exclaimed. "That's epic!"

"Well, it's not huge but it's a great space and we keep all the stuff we haven't got room for up here."

There was a little wooden ladder and a light switch on the side, which Sophie used to light up the little room underneath the hut. Hetty could see all sorts of stuff: buckets, spades, sun loungers and their cushions. There was at least one surfboard and fishing tackle in the corner as well as Jack's toys. She couldn't see the whole room from the kitchen but if it was the same size as the hut it must be quite big. "Perhaps Dad could do this with our hut," she thought. "I must remember to ask him."

"Here you are Hetty, can you lift this out for me?" Sophie lifted up a little red and yellow trike; Hetty caught hold of it and put it on the floor next to her. She watched as Sophie turned out the light, climbed up the stairs and got ready to go out.

Hetty and Jack walked to the jetty with Sophie and waved goodbye.

"Let's go and get your trike, shall we Jack?"

Hetty and Jack made their way back to the hut and said goodbye to Nigel and Dad, who said that they needed to be back by five for tea and then they set off with Jack peddling hard beside Hetty who was actually walking very slowly.

As the pair reached the café, a familiar figure appeared around the corner. It was Charlie but this time he wasn't on his own, a little girl was with him. Charlie didn't look very happy and was trying hard to ignore the child who was about seven or eight. She was trying to hold his hand.

"Hi Charlie, who's this?" Hetty ignored his obvious embarrassment and smiled at the little girl who returned her smile shyly, bending down to admire Jack's trike.

"My sister, Lucy," mumbled Charlie

"Oh she's so pretty." Hetty bent down. "I love your T-shirt Lucy, this is Jack who lives in the hut next door to mine we are just going for a walk." Jack got off his trike and started to pick up shells holding them out to Lucy who started to help him collect a few more. Hetty looked at Charlie.

"Did you know there's a party tomorrow night? It's fancy dress; everyone's going. Are you?"

Charlie looked away. "Not sure really, fancy dress is not really my thing, it depends on my grandparents, they may not let me go out in the evening; they are a bit funny like that, 'cause Mum and Dad are away."

"They can come too, it's for everyone." Hetty was surprised that she was trying to persuade him to join in. After all, he hadn't been very nice to her at junior school, but he had been concerned about her the day before when she'd bumped into him running away from the black hut. She got the feeling that he'd been frightened by the man who was lurking around, watching them.

Hetty decided she needed to know if she could trust Charlie.

"Charlie, you know that man who was asking about the children?"

"Yeah, what about him? He didn't scare me you know."

"Well..." Hetty hesitated .

"Actually," boasted Charlie, "I told him I knew everyone here and that there were no strange children, he's the only strange person I've seen here this year." Charlie sounded much braver than Hetty knew he really was.

Hetty thought for a moment or two, "But, just suppose that you had seen any children that you didn't know, would you tell him?"

"Absolutely not, I don't trust him, he's a trouble maker. Why do you ask?" Charlie seemed to be about to put two and two together.

"No reason," Hetty replied, desperate to put him off the scent. She looked around her. "Oh no, where are Jack and Lucy?"

The pair looked over to where they'd last seen the two younger children, the red and yellow trike lay on its side in the sand and there was no sign of the little girl and boy anywhere.

"JACK, JACK!" Hetty called out, panic rising in her. He couldn't be far away could he?

"Jack, where are you?" Hetty started to run down to the shoreline, looking right and left, Charlie followed her.

"Lucy!" he shouted echoing Hetty's frantic calls.

"Wait Hetty, let's stop and think. They can't have gone far." Charlie took charge.

"We were standing there by the shop and they didn't go back past us or we would have seen them, so they must have gone towards the headland." Charlie pointed in the direction of the trees.

"Ok, right, yes, let's split up and we'll ask everyone we see, they really can't have gone far, we were only talking for a little while. We'll meet again by the Noddy train station, OK?"

Hetty felt calmer. Charlie was right, they must be sensible. They can't have gone into the water as someone would have seen them. There were lots of people around. They must be ahead of them.

The youngsters split up each taking one side of the spit, stopping to ask everyone they met as they searched for their two charges. When they met at the train the two looked at each other and shook their heads, no luck, they sat down next to each other, each contemplating how they could possibly explain what had happened .

Charlie looked across to the land between the shore and the trees. Hidden in the long grass and reeds was a decrepit old rowing boat lying on its side. Charlie had an idea, he knew that Lucy loved to play hide and seek; maybe, just maybe, she was playing now.

"Hetty, the boat... let's see if they're hiding under it."

Hetty jumped up and rushed over to the boat, she bent over and crawled underneath and there, to her relief, she found the two children curled up together giggling happily.

"We won!" said Lucy "We heard you shouting but it took you ages to find us. Jack's really good at hiding, aren't you, Jack?"

Jack nodded and wriggled out from the hiding place, blinking in the bright sunlight.

"Well done Charlie. Thank goodness you were here." Hetty grinned at him with relief and decided that she did trust him enough to tell him her secret.

Hetty told him about the children as they went to retrieve Jack's trike.

"And I need to get this food to them." Hetty indicated her backpack, "I really need to move them to somewhere safer and closer to protect them from that man as I don't like him at all, will you help me?"

Charlie looked at her in amazement. "Wow, I wondered what you were up to yesterday afternoon, but I didn't think that you'd have a secret like that. Of course I'll help, we'll take the food now, what time is it?" He looked at his phone. "Half three, plenty of time, I thought it was much later than that, it seemed to take ages to find Lucy and Jack, let's swap mobile numbers so that we can stay in touch, just in case. Let's go."

The four children set off for the shed as quickly as they could. Hetty felt relieved that she had someone to share her secret with and it was much easier to get to the shed with a look out to tell her when it was all clear. She hopped over the fence and ran to the shed.

The children were so grateful for the food. They ate ravenously, even faster than Hetty had at lunchtime. Hetty tried to mime that she would come again the next day, she thought they understood and she gave them both a hug as she turned to clamber out of the window and return to Charlie, Lucy and Jack.

Chapter 10

"Oh, there you are at last, we thought you'd got lost or something. Is everything OK? Has he been a good boy?" Sophie smiled when she saw Hetty and Jack as they arrived back at the huts. Hetty hoped that she wasn't really worried and also that Jack's talk of hiding wouldn't lead Sophie to suspect that the little boy really had been missing for a while.

"Have you had a lovely time darling?" Sophie asked as she gave the little boy a hug.

"Thank you so much for looking after him Hetty, Nigel got lots of work done so you were a big help."

"Oh, that's OK," said Hetty "We had a great time, we made two new friends called Lucy and Charlie and we played hide and seek, Jack and Lucy won they hid really well, we couldn't find them anywhere!"

Hetty had decided that telling a half truth would disguise the real facts and that Sophie and Nigel would then have no real concerns about the afternoon's little adventure.

"I'll look after him anytime Sophie; I'd better go and see what Dad's up to. See you later."

Hetty hurried back to her own hut to find Dad having a break from his painting and sitting, with a glass of beer, on the veranda surveying the view again with a contented smile on his face.

"Hi Hetts, mind the wet paint. Have you had a nice afternoon? Was Jack a good boy?"

Hetty flopped down next to Dad. "Yep we had fun but I'm really tired, little children are hard work, we met a boy that I knew at the junior school, do you remember Charlie Parsons? He was horrid to me, always teasing me about my hair, asking if there were birds nesting in it, but he seems much nicer now and he has a little sister called Lucy who is really sweet."

"Well perhaps he's grown up a bit now, I'm glad you're meeting lots of new friends and having fun. I'd forgotten what a lovely place this is and knowing that you are safe messing about with friends, means that I don't have to worry about you and what you are up to." Dad ruffled Hetty's hair as he got up to get another beer.

"Would you like a drink before we have dinner?"

"Mmm, yes. Could I have a coke please?"

Dad got up to get the drinks "Where's that big bottle of coke I bought from home?"

"Oh sorry Dad, I drank it earlier."

"What? All of it?"

"I was really thirsty and I took it out with me for the afternoon. We all had some." Hetty realised that wasn't exactly true. She had shared it, just not with who Dad thought she had shared it with.

"There's only squash then. Now what shall we eat tonight? I've got some bacon and eggs or we could have sausages on the little disposable barbeque that I got yesterday. There's some salad in the cool box to go with it."

"Oh, barbeque please Dad, I'll make the salad while you do the sausages. Can we get a proper barbeque like Sophie and Nigel's?" Hetty had admired the barbeque next door with its big domed lid which she had seen Sophie using the evening before.

"Yes it's on the list Hetty, we'll go shopping tomorrow or the next day, shall we?" Dad got up to fetch the foil tray and sausages, kneeling down to find a level place to put it, "Right that'll do, now where are the matches?"

Hetty got up and found them, tossing the box down to Dad. Soon the coals were alight and the smell of the sizzling sausages was wafting up the steps and into the hut where Hetty was preparing a salad. Carefully slicing the cucumber, tomatoes, radishes, lettuce and spring onions, she divided the salad between two plates.

"Nearly ready Hetty!" Dad called up the steps "How about you?"

"Yes, ready when you are. Do you need a plate for the sausages?" Hetty took another plate down the steps and held it out while Dad piled the delicious smelling sausages onto it. The two returned to the table and ate their meal, savouring the crispy, slightly charred, meaty sausages which they dipped into ketchup and then sandwiched the whole lot into bread rolls to make hot dogs.

"Mmmm, that was yummy! I luuurve sausages, I could eat them every day!." Hetty sat back and smiled at Dad.

Just at that moment Nigel came over to the hut. He looked worried, Hetty's heart sank. What if Jack had told them something about the afternoon and she was in trouble.

"Oh, sorry to interrupt your meal." Nigel began hesitantly.

"No worries, just finished," said Dad "Is there a problem?"

"Actually, yes there is." Nigel came up the steps.

"Oh no," thought Hetty. She got up and began to clear the table.

"It's Sophie."

"Here it comes." Hetty could hardly bear to listen.

"It's her parents actually, not her, they have both been taken ill and we are going to have to go and look after them for a while. Hopefully it's not too serious but they are quite elderly. Normally they manage together when they are well but when they are ill they need some support. So, you see, we are going to have to go and stay for a few days, we were wondering if you would mind hut-sitting and keeping an eye on the place while we are gone?"

Hetty breathed a sigh of relief and looked up at Dad who was saying that it would be a pleasure to help their neighbours out. He got up with Nigel and set off over to their hut calling out to Hetty as he went.

"Just going to check out next door, Hetty. Are you coming?"

"Yep, wait for me!" she ran down to join the two men and together they made their way across to Sophie and Jack who were hurriedly packing things up. In the corner of the hut Hetty noticed a TV, which she hadn't realised was there. The early evening news was on and Hetty watched it as Dad was receiving instructions from Nigel about how to lock up and make sure that the solar panels were charging correctly to keep the fridge going.

"...and of course, please feel free to use the barbeque while we are gone, you can put some stuff in the fridge as well until you get sorted out. Oh, and please use the TV if you like."

Nigel had noticed Hetty staring at it as if she had never seen one before. But it was the news item that Hetty was absorbed in; on the screen was a lady who was pleading for her children to be returned to her. It seemed they had gone on holiday with their father and hadn't returned when they were supposed to. She was asking for the father to return them; he was apparently from another country, Turkey. Hetty watched as a photograph flashed onto the screen.

OH MY GOODNESS!

It was that man. The pieces of the puzzle started to tumble into place, the man was the children's father and they must be hiding from him. They were the two children he was so anxious to find.

Hetty looked about her, all the adults were busy, and quick as a flash she whipped out her phone and took a photograph of the picture of the man on the screen. Hetty checked it, yep it was a bit fuzzy but she thought it was reasonably clear. She looked around her; no one seemed to have noticed what she was doing. Sophie was lifting up some bags and Jack's buggy from the trap door in the centre of their kitchen and Nigel and Dad were helping her.

"If we are quick we can get the last ferry," Nigel was saying to Sophie.

"You just go; we'll lock up for you. Don't worry, everything will be fine here." Hetty thought Dad was so reassuring in a crisis. She watched as the trapdoor was lowered and a brainwave hit her with the force of a tsunami.

What an excellent place to hide the children. That was it, just right; she'd have the perfect excuse to keep popping into to check on them. She could tell Dad that she was going to watch TV or that she was getting stuff from the fridge. Dad would think that was quite normal behaviour.

She was so relieved it was as if a weight had lifted from her shoulders. Hetty and Dad helped Nigel, Sophie and Jack down to the jetty and they just caught the ferry in time.

"Don't worry everything will be fine here!" Dad called out as the ferry pulled away from the jetty.

"Yes," echoed Hetty. "Everything will be fine."

Chapter 11

When Charlie woke up the next morning he was excited. Not only was he helping to hide two children but also there was a party on the beach that evening if he could get Nana to let him go.

He sprang out of bed, threw on some clothes, grabbed a piece of toast from the table and headed for the door.

"Where are you off to in such a hurry?" asked Grandad.

"I have promised to help Hetty with some stuff this morning; I'll be back at lunchtime," he said as he headed out of the hut leaving Grandad grumbling, "Only ever here for food. Uses the place like a hotel."

Charlie could just hear Nana laughing and saying Grandad was young once.

It was a beautiful summer day and Charlie had a spring in his step.

"Come on Charlie," called out Hetty who was already waiting outside her hut for him. Bob was there sitting quietly at her feet.

"I've got some food for Kaya and Hasan, we need to get going as they are bound to be hungry and I've got something really important to tell you."

As they walked towards the wooded area, Hetty described what she had seen on the TV in Sophie and Nigel's hut the evening before.

"So these children's Dad kidnapped them but they escaped and are hiding out somewhere. It must be Kaya and Hasan," said Charlie, putting two and two together.

"I couldn't really tell from the fuzzy photos on the screen, they looked a bit younger, but there was quite a clear one of their Dad which I took a picture of on my phone. I thought we could show it to Kaya and Hasan to see if they recognise him," said Hetty.

"Show me the picture, quick."

Hetty got her phone out and showed Charlie.

"Hmm, it's not very clear but it could be him."

"Oi, What you two doing?" A deep, strange sounding voice called out from behind them. As they turned around they saw the man a few metres away, heading in their direction.

Hetty quickly put her phone safely in her pocket.

"Walking our dog, why, what's it to you?" said Charlie with as much courage as he could muster.

He saw Hetty glance at him with a mixture of admiration and fear.

"You always around here. Why that?"

"Our dog loves this bit of his walk. He likes to chase the rabbits," said Charlie

Hetty seemed to have lost the power of speech.

"Have you seen two kids around here?" asked the man.

"You've asked us before and we've already told you that we haven't. Who are these children and why are you looking for them?" asked Charlie

"Not your business. If you see them, you tell me."

"Why should we?" said Charlie

"Because if I find out you seen them and you not told me I will be very angry… very, very angry," growled the man.

"Come on Bob, let's get on with your walk." Hetty seemed to have found her voice.

Charlie and Hetty walked on down the track away from the man. They didn't dare look around to see if he was watching them or following.

"I really don't like him, he is scary," said Hetty

"Yes, we need to stay away from him. Is he following? Let's head into the woods and then we can check and see where he is."

They left the track and doubled back on themselves but there was no sign of the man.

"Come on, we had better hurry," said Hetty.

They reached the shed where the children were hiding and Hetty climbed in the window to give them the food, whilst Charlie kept a lookout.

The children were so pleased to see Hetty and Bob. They ate their food quickly and whilst Kaya was on the floor stroking Bob, who was loving all the attention, Hetty showed the photo she had on her phone to Hasan.

He grabbed the phone and the colour seemed to drain from his face. He became really agitated and started packing their few bits together and grabbing his sister.

"WAIT, WAIT! What are you doing?" asked Hetty

He was talking quickly to his sister in their native tongue. She shrieked and jumped up.

"STOP. No, you are safe, it's OK," said Hetty, holding her hands up to prevent them running away.

Hetty realised that she and Charlie were right to presume that the man in the photo was their dad. She desperately needed to convince them to stay where they were for the time being.

She pointed around the inside of the hut and smiled saying, "Safe here, stay. Safe here, stay. OK?".

The two children spoke for a long time together until, almost with a sigh of resignation, Hasan nodded and put their belongings down on the floor of the hut.

Hetty mimed her leaving, the sun going down and her coming back again with food. Hasan nodded and gave Hetty a hug.

Hetty texted Charlie to make sure the coast was clear. She climbed out of the window and quickly went back to where Charlie was waiting.

Bob seemed to have his own way of getting in and out of the hut as he was already there with Charlie.

"How are they?"

"Well, it is definitely their dad. They were terrified by the picture. I thought they were going to run away. I think we are going to have to move them but it will be risky."

"Where to and how?" said Charlie.

"I think I know where we can hide them. Sophie and Nigel from the hut next door to mine have gone away for a week and they have a trap door in the floor, which leads to a basement room underneath the kitchen. It would be a perfect hiding place for them as I could nip in regularly to check they are OK. It's even got a portable camping toilet in there that they use for Jack. I just don't know how we can move them without being seen."

"Simple,." said Charlie. "It's the fancy dress party tonight. If we dress them up as ghosts, no one would know who was underneath the sheets."

"Oh Charlie you are brilliant. That's a great idea!" exclaimed Hetty.

Charlie blushed, pleased that Hetty liked his idea.

The two conspirators were deep in conversation when they came around the corner a few huts away from Hetty's.

"Hetty, stop!" said Charlie. "Look!"

She looked down the line of huts and saw her dad sitting outside, chatting to none other than Hasan and Kaya's father.

"What's he doing?" asked Hetty.

"No idea, but it looks like he is leaving."

The two men stood up and shook hands. The other man strode off down the beach.

Charlie, Hetty and Bob made sure he had completely disappeared before they approached Hetty's hut.

"Hey Dad, who was that?" asked Hetty.

"Someone called Smith, I think. Seems an odd name for someone who struggles to speak English. He wanted to tell me that he had caught Charlie snooping around his hut and he was warning me that Charlie was no good. He suggested that I should stop you spending so much time with him. I don't think I liked him very much," said Dad.

"But Dad, Charlie is my friend and he helped me look after Jack."

"Oh, don't worry. I don't intend to take any notice. There's something a little strange about that man. You two had better stay out of his way."

"We will certainly do that," said Hetty.

"I had better get off, Hetty. I will ask my grandparents if they have any old sheets that we can use for the fancy dress tonight," he said with a wink. "If I come by at about six... is that OK?"

"Perfect, see you then."

Charlie ran off back to his grandparents' hut only to find out that 'Mr Smith' had also paid them a visit.

"He says you've been snooping. We told him that kids see this as a place for adventures and that was a good thing but he wasn't very happy. I think he thought we should be telling you off. Bit of an odd fellow. Very funny accent. I'm not sure I liked him," said Grandad

"Horrible man," said Nana who didn't ever hold back on her opinions. "Better stay out of his way."

"I will, promise," said Charlie happily.

"Nana, can I go to the fancy dress party on the beach tonight please? Everyone else is going, it's just at the café."

"If you like but what are you going to wear?" asked Nana.

"Hetty and I thought we would go as ghosts. Have you any old sheets?"

"There are plenty from last year that I meant to throw away. Help yourself, they are in the box marked 'linen' in the roof room."

"Thanks Nana," said Charlie as he disappeared inside.

Chapter 12

It was almost six o'clock and Hetty was in the hut next door. She'd told Dad she was going to check on the fridge and put some coke and beer in it to get cold but really she was checking on the trapdoor. In the cellar area were a couple of blankets and an old mattress, so that was OK. She had taken some food supplies and water. The camping toilet seemed to be OK as well, luxury really after the old shed where they had been hiding.

Footsteps came up the steps outside the hut. Hetty jumped and quickly climbed out of the cellar, she was just lowering the trap door when she heard someone call out.

"Hello anyone there?" Hetty recognised Charlie's voice and she ran to the front door.

"Quick, come in and see what you think." Hetty proudly showed Charlie the hiding place.

"It's perfect Hetty, let's go get them, I've got the costumes look." Charlie showed Hetty the sheets which he had found in the linen box.

The two children set off, Hetty carefully locking up behind them and calling goodbye to Dad. Dad was asleep on the veranda and oblivious to the world. Hetty wasn't sure whether to keep the key to Sophie and Nigel's hut or put it back in her own hut. What if Dad decided to check it or get himself a beer, she decided to keep the key because then at least Dad couldn't go in and she could always pretend that she had forgotten to put it back. She was amazed at how easily she was finding it to deceive people and tell white lies to hide what was going on.

"Did you get four sheets, Charlie?" Hetty had a sudden thought .

"Sure did, why?" Charlie looked at her and held the bundle of sheets out to her.

"Well, I think we should put ours on now so that if we see 'Smith' he won't know who we are, it'll be like a cloak of invisibility like Harry Potter's." Hetty held her hand out for a sheet.

"That is a great idea." Charlie gave her a sheet and selected one for himself. Quickly they shrouded themselves in white and found the two slits which Charlie had cut out so they could see where they were going.

They reached the 'Keep Out' sign with no problems, people who passed them smiled and one or two lads called after them making what they thought were ghostly haunting noises but other than that the journey was quite easy.

Once at the fence they decided to disrobe in order to climb over the fence more easily. Hetty went first with Charlie keeping watch and then Hetty looked out while Charlie clambered over. The two ran swiftly to the shed and around the side so they were out of sight of the pathway. Hetty climbed onto the tree stump and held the window open, climbing in as she had done before, Charlie followed her.

"Hello Hasan, Kaya., It's me, Hetty."

The two children emerged from the shadows and then shied back when they saw Charlie. Hasan shielded his sister behind him.

"It's OK, this is Charlie, my friend." Hetty pointed at Charlie and said again, "Friend."

Charlie smiled in what he hoped was a reassuring way.

"How are we going to make them understand that we need to move them?" questioned Charlie.

"Leave that to me." Hetty got her phone out and showed the picture of the man to the children. She put the phone on the floor to show them that he could come to the shed.

Hasan and Kaya looked worried and Hasan started to pack up their belongings.

Charlie, pointed to the window and held out the sheets to the children. He put a sheet over his head to show them how they would be hidden.

Hetty then tried to show them with gestures that they were going to move somewhere safer. She indicated that they would all need to climb out of the window.

Hasan seemed to understand and started speaking quickly to his sister. He packed their few bits and pieces up into his backpack and got ready to leave.

"Perfect. Now let us get out of here." Charlie and Hetty took off the sheets and bundled them out of the window. Then, one by one, all four clambered out and got dressed up. Hasan looked a slightly different shape to the others as he also had his backpack on with the few belongings he and his sister had with them.

This was going to be the hard part, getting all of them back onto the path without being seen. Hetty and Charlie put their fingers to their lips and said, "Sshh!"

Hasan and Kaya nodded, understanding that they must be quiet.

Hetty peered around the shed, she saw the Noddy train engine appear, chugging along towards the car park, she dodged back to their hiding place.

"We need a plan Charlie, have you got your phone?"

"Of course I have," Charlie replied

"Well, you go first and get over the fence then text when the coast is clear. I will wait here with Hasan and Kaya, when you text I will bring each of them over one at a time. What do you think?" Hetty's heart was pounding she really hadn't thought this through but this might just work.

"OK. Good idea, but I'm going to take this sheet off for this bit." With that, Charlie peered around the corner, listening intently. When he judged it to be all clear, he ran off, swiftly vaulted over the fence and then quickly shrugged the sheet over his head and leant back on the fence trying to look as relaxed and as carefree as it was possible for a ghost to look.

No one was about, so Charlie texted 'all clear' to Hetty. From around the corner of the shed two more ghosts appeared and ran as quickly as possible to Charlie, Hetty helped the small ghost, Kaya, to climb up the fence and Charlie found her hand under the sheet and helped her down the other side. Hetty ran back to Hasan.

Kaya and Charlie looked up and down the path, Charlie could hear voices and Kaya shrank behind him and sank to the ground. A young couple came around the bend, they were holding hands and laughing, they had eyes only for each other and didn't take any notice of the two ghosts next to the fence. As they disappeared from view Charlie strained his ears, he really couldn't hear anything except the wind rustling in the trees and the sound of a gull screeching in the distance. He re-sent his text and the last two ghosts ran as quickly as they could to the fence. Hasan was over in a flash and Hetty followed him onto the path.

The four children set off as quickly as they could back to the beach huts. Kaya was holding tightly onto Hasan's hand with Charlie leading the way. The Noddy train came past with a few more fancy dress characters on board. A fairy and a wizard waved cheerily; Hetty and Charlie made haunting noises back as they followed the train.

As they walked Hetty set her mind another problem, that of getting the children into the hut. They couldn't very well just march up the steps in full view of Dad and anyone else who was around, they'd have to get the children in through the back door. Hetty formed her plan and then told Charlie.

"Charlie, when we get back you take the children to the back of the hut and keep out of sight, I'll go and distract Dad and make an excuse to go next door, then I'll open the back door and we can get them into the cellar, do you think that will work?"

"I hadn't even thought about it Hetty, I think it's a good plan. Let's do it."

And so the four of them returned to the huts with Charlie and Hetty splitting up. Whilst Charlie took Hasan and Kaya around the back of the huts, Hetty went up to the door of her hut and stood outside waving her arms up and down making ghostly noises.

Dad looked up from his newspaper and pretended to be scared.

"Great costume, Hetty."

"Oh, how did you know it was me, Dad?" Hetty laughed.

"Just a guess. You must be thirsty after all that haunting. Do you fancy a drink?" asked Dad.

Hetty offered to get Dad a beer and some coke for herself from the fridge next door. Luckily, Dad hadn't noticed that the key was missing; in fact he'd only just woken up from his nap.

Next door Hetty's plan worked brilliantly and the children made themselves comfortable in the cellar, eating and drinking the food that Hetty had put there earlier and looking more relaxed and happy than she had ever seen them.

Chapter 13

After Hetty had given Dad his beer she and Charlie walked off down the beach, in their ghost costumes.

The sense of relief that both Hetty and Charlie felt that the move had gone so well was immense and walking around in their costumes meant that even if they bumped into Mr Smith, he would not know it was them.

"No sign of him at the moment," said Charlie.

"Perhaps he's gone away for a while," suggested Hetty hopefully.

"Somehow I doubt it."

They turned the corner and headed in the direction of the beach BBQ.

Two characters were on the path ahead of them.

It was Megs and Danni. Well at least Hetty thought it was them. "Is that you?" Hetty asked. "Your costumes are amazing."

The two girls had found some costume make up and had turned themselves into very scary-looking witches.

"Who is that under there then? Is that you Hetty?"

"Yep, and me," said Charlie.

"Yes it is us," confirmed Megs. "These costumes have taken us all day to make but it was good fun. Oh look, isn't it beautiful!"

Hetty stopped and looked at the view in front of her. The beach had been turned into a magical place.

There were about 40 people, all dressed up as pirates, mermaids, fairies, fishermen and, strangely, one Justin Beiber lookalike that turned out to be Ryan.

Even the beach had been dressed up and decorated with jars with candles in. The light was just starting to fade and the whole beach looked beautiful. In the distance you could see the rocky outcrop of the Needles at the end of the Isle of Wight. The sky was a glorious reddy-orange colour as the sun dipped below the horizon.

Some of the beach huts close by were decorated with strings of twinkling fairy lights around the outside. The sound of people laughing and chatting rose up above the music that was coming from the speakers outside the café.

"Oh it looks so lovely. A magical wonderland!" exclaimed Hetty. "This is going to be fun."

"Come on, let's check out the food, I'm starving," said Megs as she headed off towards the BBQ pulling Hetty along with her.

They sat on the beach eating their burgers - Charlie, Hetty, Megs, Danni, Ryan and Bob who was hoping for some scraps.

When the food was finished there was a competition for the best costume. Megs and Danni were voted as joint winners.

"What's your prize?" asked Hetty.

"Ten free ice cream vouchers and this cup," said Megs, proudly holding it up.

Charlie came up alongside Hetty asking, "Any sign of him?"

"No, not even a glimpse, thank goodness."

"Come on you lot, it's time to light the sky lanterns," said Justin, the owner of the café.

"What lanterns?" asked Hetty.

"You'll see," said Megs. "It's an annual tradition, you will love it."

They all followed Justin and collected a large cylinder of material that had a small candle attached at its base. The children took one between two of them to the water's edge. They held them up whilst Justin lit each candle and when they felt a pull, they released the lantern into the night sky.

Hetty lay on the beach looking up at the darkness, watching as the lanterns floated silently up and up and up. There must have been about 20 of them. It was a beautiful sight, something Hetty had never seen before.

"This is such a special place, isn't it Hetty?"

Hetty looked up to see her dad standing there.

He came and lay down on the sand next to Hetty.

"I love this place Dad, this is the best summer ever." said Hetty.

"It is certainly an amazing sight," said Dad.

They lay there for ages just watching the lanterns as they faded away, carried by the light evening breeze.

Hetty wished Hasan and Kaya could have been there as well. She knew the children were safe at the moment but what would happen next? Hetty shivered.

Chapter 14

"Come on Hetty, you can't spend all day asleep."

Hetty was in the middle of a very strange dream, full of shadows that she couldn't quite make out. Dark figures floated in and out; she tried to scream but where was her voice? She thought she heard Dad calling to her but his voice seemed such a long way away. As the dream faded his voice became louder.

"Come on sleepy head, it's a beautiful day and you've already slept through half of the morning."

Hetty woke suddenly as the words became clearer. She sat bolt upright, her heart was pounding.

"What's the time?"

"Eleven, you must have been really tired last night."

Oh no, what about Hasan and Kaya? At that moment she heard her phone bleep.

"You are popular today! That must be about the fifth time it's beeped in the last hour," said Dad

Hetty grabbed her phone and saw she had missed a couple of calls from Charlie. There were also a number of texts, which got more and more urgent with each one that she read. The final one said: 'I don't know what's going on so am on my way over to check u r ok. C.'

"That's a worried face. Is there a problem Hetts?" said Dad.

Hetty smiled as brightly as she could. "Oh no, nothing wrong, just my friends chatting about last night and Charlie is on his way over. I forgot I arranged to meet him this morning. I can't believe I slept so long. Can I just grab some breakfast?"

"Help yourself, I am just nipping to the shop for some bits. I won't be long," said Dad.

Just at that moment Charlie arrived.

"Morning Mr Webster. Is Hetty around?"

"Hi Charlie. Yes, the sleepy head has finally woken up, go on in, she's just having breakfast. Oh and Charlie, Mike will do rather than Mr Webster."

"OK, thanks Mike."

And with that Hetty's Dad strode off in the direction of the shop.

"You had me worried when you didn't answer your phone this morning, I thought Smith might have got you."

"Oh sorry Charlie, I don't know what happened but I only just woke up. Come on Charlie, we need to nip next door and check on Hasan and Kaya before Dad gets back. Grab that cereal and milk. Quick!"

They took the key and ran out of Hetty's hut.

Hetty who was in front stopped abruptly on the porch. She stopped so fast that Charlie collided with her.

"Ouch Hetty what do you think you are doing!" yelped Charlie

"Look Charlie, it's him."

Charlie looked at where Hetty was pointing. He saw 'Smith' down by the ferry talking to Sam.

"Let's get in next door and hopefully he won't see us."

They let themselves into Sophie and Nigel's hut, closed the curtains and lifted the floor hatch.

"Make sure you lock the door from the inside Charlie," said Hetty who was worried about Smith.

Hasan and Kaya climbed out of the basement room looking relieved to be out of their hiding place. Hungrily they tucked into the breakfast of cereal and milk. Hetty noticed that Kaya didn't look very well; her face seemed pale and sweaty. She wasn't sure how to ask Kaya if she was OK, so she put her hand on Kaya's forehead to check her temperature just as Hetty's mum had done to her whenever Hetty felt poorly. Her forehead felt a little clammy but Kaya just smiled and carried on with her breakfast. Hetty thought that it was probably because she had been cooped up in the basement room for so long.

As soon as their breakfast was finished, Hetty and Charlie cleared everything away.

"Do you think it will be safe enough for the children to stay in the main bit of the hut as long as we keep the curtains closed?" asked Charlie.

"I don't see why not as long as I keep the key with me so that Dad can't get in and they stay away from the windows," replied Hetty. "It is so much easier having them so close."

"We will be back later to check you are OK and bring you some more food," Hetty explained as they locked the door.

"Don't go near the windows," Said Charlie as he pointed to the windows and shook his head vigorously. Hasan seemed to understand.

Hetty and Charlie got back just before Hetty's dad came in through the rear door.

"Have you any plans today Hetts? Did you know that there is a treasure hunt going on today?" asked Dad

"That sounds like great fun," Said Charlie "What do you think, Hetty? Shall we have a go?"

"Good idea Charlie. We'll be back later Dad. Is that OK?"

"Of course, I've never known you to spend so much time outside. It will do you good. Don't go too far though."

"Thanks Dad, see you later!" Hetty gave her Dad a hug and she and Charlie went off down the beach.

"I have an idea Charlie but you may not like it."

"What are you planning now?" asked Charlie.

"I think we should go and check out 'Smith''s hut. There may be some evidence about why he is so convinced that the children are somewhere around here. Why else would he still be nosing around here and questioning everybody about them?"

Charlie didn't look too happy about the suggestion but he nodded. "I suppose so."

"Come on but keep an eye out for him," said Hetty.

* * *

They walked past the black hut a couple of times, but there was no sign of 'Smith'.

Hetty was feeling brave. "Let's have a closer look."

Carefully walking all around the hut, they came to the door.

"Wow, that's the biggest padlock I've ever seen." Charlie pointed to a huge black rusty lock that was holding the doors together. "It's also got the weirdest pattern on the lock, have a look at this."

The lock had a swirly pattern engraved in the metal. "That's odd, locks are usually smooth." Something about those markings looked familiar. "Hang on a minute, I've seen this before. Bob found a key last week. I thought he'd dug it up from somewhere but maybe he pinched it from here. It's really big, old and rusty and I am sure it matches this lock," said Hetty.

"Where is it? Have you still got it?" asked Charlie, excitedly.

"It's in my hut. It's in a drawer, let's see if it fits."

They ran back to Hetty's and burst into the hut.

"Hey, slow down you two, where's the fire?" exclaimed Dad

"Sorry Mr... er... Mike, we are trying to find some bits for the treasure hunt," said Charlie

Hetty looked at him, impressed by his quick thinking.

"Can we take the old key that Bob found last week, please?"

"Sure, help yourself. Hetty, it's nearly lunchtime. Do you want to have something to eat before you disappear off or will you have it later?" asked Dad.

"I'm not hungry yet, thanks Dad. We'll be back in about an hour. See you later." And with that the two of them headed off in the direction of the black hut.

"I wonder where he is. I think it might be best for me to nip in and have a look inside if the key fits and you keep a lookout for 'Smith'," said Hetty.

"What signal shall I use if he comes along?"

"Can you whistle?" asked Hetty.

"No, not really, what about if I throw a stick or a stone at the side of the hut? It would make a loud enough sound. Hetty…"

"That should work."

"You will be careful, won't you? He's not a nice man."

"I'll be careful, come on let's see if this key fits." said Hetty, anxious to get inside and explore.

They were watching the door of the black hut from a short distance away to make sure the coast was clear. There had been no sign of 'Smith' since they spotted him talking to Sam by the ferry.

"Here goes," said Hetty as she ran towards the hut and tried the key in the lock. The key went in easily but didn't seem to want to turn. "It's not working," said Hetty

"Here, let me have a go, you keep a lookout." Charlie was nervous but he was determined to help. He wiggled the key a few times, the padlock opened and he realised it had been open all along. "That's it, it's open," said Charlie excitedly.

"Oh, well done Charlie, you are brilliant!"

Charlie puffed his chest out with pride.

"You go and keep lookout and I will be as quick as I can," said Hetty as she slipped inside the dark, dingy hut.

Slowly her eyes became used to the darkness and there were a few streaks of light that came through the gaps in the hut. The hut was full of all sorts of fishing paraphernalia. There were boxes full of old fishing lines, lobster pots and things that looked like floats. Yuk, it really smelt horrible.

Hetty started to move around the hut, careful not to disturb anything.

She looked behind the lobster pots but couldn't see anything of any interest. One corner of the hut had a blanket in it, a pillow and there were remnants of food and cups of cold drinks.

"So this must be where he is sleeping," thought Hetty.

She moved off to the far corner of the hut. Something bright caught her eye, she moved closer and picked up what she had seen. It was a soft toy, a rabbit. Hetty had seen the eyes that were reflected in the sunlight coming through the cracks in the blacked out windows. She checked around this part of the hut and found some more bedding and a couple of children's books.

Hetty quickly put everything back in place and started to move across the hut towards the door when she heard a THUD on the outside of the hut.

"What you doing?" shouted a familiar voice.

"Oh no!" thought Hetty. "It's him!" She looked around quickly for somewhere to hide.

"Who me? I'm throwing stones at this hut," she heard Charlie shout back.

"This my hut, you stop that and come here. I told you stay away. You not listened."

THUD

"I say stop, you..."

Hetty couldn't make out what he said next. It was in a different language.

Her heart was pumping, how was she going to get out of here?

THUD

"Right, you in big trouble now, come here!" shouted 'Smith'.

"You've got to catch me first!" challenged Charlie.

Hetty couldn't hear anything now. She didn't know if they were still outside, or if Smith had got Charlie but she realised that she couldn't stay in the hut.

She listened intently as she slowly opened the door. Would he be waiting for her on the other side. She had to be brave and risk it.

The door creaked open as she peered out.

No one was there.

Hetty locked the hut, put the key in her pocket and ran as fast as she could away from the hut towards the beach.

She couldn't see Charlie or 'Smith' anywhere.

Hetty daren't call for Charlie in case 'Smith' was nearby.

She headed to Charlie's hut but as she came close she could see 'Smith' talking to Charlie's grandparents.

They called to Hetty.

"Hetty, this man said our Charlie has just been throwing stones at his hut, do you know where he is?" asked Charlie's Nana with a look of dislike directed at 'Smith'.

Hetty thought quickly "Can't have been Charlie, he's been with me all morning. I just left him at the beach so I could go for lunch. He'll be back in a minute."

"There you see, I told you it wasn't Charlie. We don't appreciate your coming here trying to get him into trouble. Please stop bothering us." said Charlie's Grandad.

'Smith' walked off muttering to himself. As soon as he was out of sight Charlie came around from the back of the hut.

"I thought you were headed home for lunch, Hetty," Charlie said, slyly winking at her with a grin on his face.

"Yep, I'm on my way. Why don't you pop round this afternoon and we can carry on with our treasure hunt?" said Hetty. She was eager to tell Charlie what she had seen and to thank him for drawing Smith away.

"I've got a couple of jobs for you to do first, young man. You slipped off this morning without doing them." said Charlie's Nana

"Text me," said Charlie as Hetty started back to her hut. She was very late for lunch; her stomach was growling at her. She hoped Hasan and Kaya were OK.

Chapter 15

Hetty arrived back at her hut just as she got a call from Dad asking where she was.

"I'm here," she called out.

"Well, better late than never Hetty. I've made you some lunch but it's probably gone cold now," said Dad.

Hetty walked over to the table and picked up a plate of cheese salad sandwiches.

"Ha, ha, very funny Dad!"

Dad smiled and put down the paintbrush that seemed to have been fixed to his hand all morning.

Hetty looked around. "The hut is looking great, Dad. It is going to look like new by the time we have finished with it. I'm starving. Are there any more of these?" asked Hetty

"You haven't even started those yet. I don't know where you are putting it all. You are eating enough for both of us," said Dad

"Sorry Dad, I think it's all this fresh air."

"You eat that up and then we'll see if you are still hungry."

Hetty was getting quite good at pretending to eat her meals whilst hiding some of it to take to Hasan and Kaya.

She ended up with two spare sandwiches hidden in her backpack but couldn't find a way to get away and take them to the children next door. Dad seemed to be watching her very closely. Maybe he was catching on to her slightly odd behaviour.

This could be a problem.

Beep

It was Charlie texting to find out what she had seen in the hut.

Hetty sat on their porch and replied: 'Found bed and kids stuff. Must be H and K. Can't get out. Dad suspicious. Need to deliver food. Any ideas?'

'Will finish here and call by. Will think of something. C'

"Who's that text from Hetty?" asked Dad who had come out of the hut and was standing behind her.

"Just Charlie. He's coming over in a bit."

"You two seem to be spending a lot of time together," said Dad

"Yes I really like him but we do meet up with the others as well,." said Hetty trying to make Dad feel everything was normal.

"You would tell me if you had a problem wouldn't you, Hetts?" said Dad.

"You would be the first to know, Dad," said Hetty, feeling that actually that was quite true. She didn't like to keep secrets from her dad but at the moment she felt the fewer people that knew about Hasan and Kaya the better.

"Good, well I've promised to collect Grace's chair this afternoon from Bournemouth. She loves that old rocking chair of hers but it's ancient and has been repaired. I will be quite a while, will you be OK? When I get back, perhaps you and Charlie could help me make the supper this evening. I bumped into Charlie's grandparents earlier and they said it would be OK for him to eat with us tonight. I have asked them to keep an eye out for you this afternoon whilst I am away. OK?"

"Yes, thanks Dad, I will be fine, see you later."

As soon as her Dad had gone, Hetty gathered up her backpack with the sandwiches in, added some drinks and crisps. She let herself into the hut next door, there was no sign of Hasan and Kaya. They must be keeping out of sight. She closed the door behind her and just as she did that there was a loud knock that made Hetty jump. She slowly peeked around the curtain and saw with relief that it was just Charlie.

"Charlie, you scared me!"

"Sorry Hetty, let me in, I don't want to see 'Smith' again today if I can help it."

Hetty opened the door and locked it quickly.

"Charlie you did so well earlier drawing him away from the hut. I don't know how I would have got out of there otherwise."

"No probs, we're partners looking out for each other in this."

They looked around but there was no sign of the two children.

"Hasan… Kaya… where are you?" whispered Hetty.

The trapdoor was still open; Charlie peered into the darkness below.

Hasan's face appeared in the entrance looking worried and beckoning to them.

Charlie and Hetty followed Hasan down the steps into the basement room. Kaya was curled up on the floor in the corner.

"What's the matter with Kaya?" Asked Charlie

Hasan touched his forehead and took it off quickly as if he had been burnt.

"She has got a temperature. I thought she looked ill this morning. What shall we do?" asked Hetty worriedly.

"Let's give them the food and a drink and see if that makes any difference," suggested Charlie

"Ok, you do that. I'm worried about her. I think we need help but Dad will be gone all afternoon. What about asking your grandparents for some advice? You could pretend that it is you that is ill and see what they suggest."

Charlie stopped in the middle of handing the food to Hasan.

"I don't think that is a very good idea as they will ask too many questions and stop me coming out again. Their usual response is to send me to bed."

Hetty thought for a while. She looked over at Kaya who seemed to be getting weaker and had not eaten any of the food in front of her.

Hetty poured out a glass of water and tried to get Kaya to sip it but Kaya just lay on the mattress shivering.

"What are we going to do Charlie? She looks really ill to me."

"When you showed me that photo of 'Smith', was there a phone number at the bottom?" asked Charlie.

"I think there was, let's check," said Hetty as she got her phone out of her pocket. "You're right Charlie, there is a number."

Hetty rang the number but it was an answering machine asking you to leave contact details and information you might have about the two missing children and their father.

She left a message saying that she may have some information about the missing children; she left her mobile number but decided not to leave her name.

Now all they had to do was wait.

"Look, Kaya is asleep," Charlie said.

"We had better go but I think we need to check on her every hour," said Hetty who also showed Hasan on her watch that they would be back in an hour.

Hasan looked grateful; he was obviously quite worried about his sister.

"I think we had better go out the back way Hetty as there are a lot of people around at the front and we don't want to make people curious,." said Charlie, peering out from behind the curtains.

"Good idea." said Hetty, as they headed out the rear door, locking it behind them.

Chapter 16

Hetty hadn't slept well at all, and when she woke on Thursday morning she was worried about Kaya, she really hadn't looked very well last night when Hetty had checked on her before bedtime. She had to get to the hut next door as soon as she could. Hetty peered over the side of the bunk - no Dad, he must have got up already and be at the showers, Hetty quickly pulled on some clothes and jumped down from the ladder, if she was quick she could get to the children before he got back. Just as she got to the door Dad appeared.

"Morning Hett, how are you today? I thought we could go into town today to stock up and buy a barbeque. What do you think?"

Hetty thought quickly. "Um, well I didn't sleep too well actually Dad, I think I've got a headache coming on, but you go, I'll just have a rest here if you don't mind."

"Do you need a tablet for your head, sweetheart. I've got some somewhere; let me see, they might be in the kitchen drawer." Dad looked worried and started to rummage in the drawer. "Well I don't have to go to town today, we could go tomorrow instead, ah, here we are." He held up the packet of tablets triumphantly "Now I think you should only have one at your age." He read the instructions carefully. "Yes one will be fine and we'll see how you are later."

Hetty had to play this carefully. With Dad out of the way it would be much easier to check on the children and hopefully the helpline would contact her this morning so she would not need to involve Dad.

"Oh, I'll be OK, Dad. Maybe Grace could pop in and make sure that I'm alright if it makes you happier," Hetty suggested helpfully.

"Great idea, if you are sure you will be OK. Let's have breakfast and I'll go and see her."

Dad had filled the kettle on the way back from his shower, he lit the gas to make the tea and Hetty made her way to the showers, glancing at the next door hut as she went. All seemed quiet but she still worried about what was happening inside.

After breakfast Dad went to find Grace who, as luck would have it, was just coming around the corner. As she needed some supplies from town she was happy to keep an eye on Hetty in exchange for Dad getting her bits and pieces.

"She'll be fine don't you worry Mr Webster, I'll make sure of it," Grace assured Dad

"Please call me Mike," said Dad smiling cheerfully as he bent down to give Bob a pat on the head.

"Mike it is then. Now, off you go and don't forget my cod liver oil and peppermints."

"I certainly won't," laughed Dad "What a weird combination!"

After Dad had left, Hetty packed up some food and the tablets that Dad had found and she took the key for next door. She was about to leave when her phone rang. Quickly she closed the door to her hut; if this was who she thought it was she didn't want anyone to hear her conversation.

"Hello, this is the missing person helpline, I believe you contacted us last night with information about two missing children? My name is George Watts and I am a police liaison officer. Could you tell me what you know please, you don't have to give your name but it would be helpful if you did."

The man sounded really friendly and Hetty felt so relieved to be able to share her knowledge with an official person that she gave her name and told the man everything that had happened so far.

The man listened to everything that Hetty had to say and when she had finished he said, "Well, Hetty, you have been very helpful and sensible in not letting the man who has been asking about the children know their whereabouts. What we need to do is establish that these are the children we are looking for. So could you take a photograph of them to send to me?"

"Yes, yes no problem I was just going to see them, I'll be about five minutes, OK?"

"Good, can you send them to this number please, speak to you soon, bye."

Hetty hurried over to next door and unlocking the door she checked that no one was watching and let herself in. She peered down through the open hatch to see the children's faces looking up at her, Hasan seemed to be trying to smile when he saw her. He looked over to where his sister was still curled up in the corner. Kaya didn't look well at all and Hetty put her hand on the girl's forehead; she felt hot and clammy and her eyes looked really dull. Hetty gave them the food and drink that she had brought and opened the headache tablets. Should she give Kaya a tablet? What if it made her worse? Hetty really wasn't sure what to do, maybe she'd ask the nice George Watts man what to do when she sent the pictures.

Hetty got her phone out as Hasan tried to get Kaya to eat something. Just as she prepared to take the picture there was a knock on the door., Hasan looked at her and froze. Hetty put her fingers to her lips and Hasan nodded. Hetty crept up the steps and over to the window, pulling back a corner of the curtain.

It was Charlie standing at the door so Hetty quickly opened up and let him in, locking the door behind him.

"It's OK Hasan, it's Charlie."

Hetty explained to Charlie about the helpline and needing to send pictures to the policeman. Charlie helped Hasan to get Kaya up the steps so that they could get a clear picture of both children. Hasan seemed to understand the word police when Hetty tried to explain what she was doing. They sent the photo off using Hetty's phone, hoping for a quick response.

Whilst they waited Hetty asked Charlie what he thought about giving Kaya a tablet.

"Well she certainly doesn't look good, but I'm not sure. What if she's allergic to something? Hopefully the police will get here quickly and they can decide."

BANG! BANG!

"YOU IN THERE, OPEN DOOR." The voice was loud and the banging ferocious, the four children looked at each other in horror. Just at that moment Hetty's phone rang.

"Hi, is that Hetty? It's George Watts here."

"Yes," whispered Hetty. "It's me."

"Just confirming that the pictures you took are of the children we are looking for, could you tell me where you are please and we'll get to you as soon as we can."

BANG! BANG!

"COME OUT NOW!" The man shouted even louder.

"What is that?" George asked.

"It's the man who is looking for the children, he's found us. Please, please come quickly we are at Hengistbury Head in beach hut 66, it's not far from the jetty. Hurry please."

"Hetty, stay on the phone. Don't hang up." George was clearly very worried but the phone went dead. Hetty was out of battery and her charger was next door.

Charlie was closing the trap door where the children had returned, clearly unhappy and frightened.

"Charlie have you got your phone with you? I'm out of battery and the police want us to stay in touch," Hetty asked anxiously

"Yes, what's the number?" Charlie got his phone out ready to ring but the banging on the door was more insistent and suddenly the children realised that it was coming from the back door not the front. Charlie looked around and started to move whatever he could to barricade the door.

Hetty ran to the front door and looked out, she was so frightened what should they do? Could she get out the front and lock up behind her and run for help before 'Smith' realised she'd gone? Or should they stay put and wait for the police to come.

As she looked out she saw a very welcome sight, it was a tricycle with Grace pedalling as hard as she could. Hetty ran up the ladder to the bedroom. She crawled over to the little window in the eaves of the roof and opened it as wide as she could.

"Grace! Grace!" she called.

Grace stopped and looked all around her.

"Up here Grace!"

Grace looked up at last. "Hetty, what on earth is going on? What is all that shouting about and what are you doing in Sophie and Nigel's hut?"

"Grace, we need help, I can't explain now but the man at the back of the hut is trying to get in. You have to stop him, please help us." Hetty was pleading for help and Grace was just the person to ask. Grace looked around her.

"Don't you worry dear I'll be back." Grace pedalled off just as 'Smith' reappeared at the front. He looked up at the window and shook his fist at Hetty.

"You let me in!"

"NO!" shouted Hetty. "GO AWAY!"

The man came closer, towards the steps of the hut.

Out of the corner of her eye Hetty saw Grace returning carrying an enormous paddle. Quickly Hetty realised that she must distract the man and not let him turn and see Grace.

"Why do you want us to let you in?" she shouted to him.

"You got my kids!" the man shouted back. Just at that moment Grace heaved the paddle with all her might and hit him on the head. The man fell in slow motion, just like a tree being felled, face first onto the sand and Grace, quick as a flash, sat on his back.

"Quick!" Grace called. "Get help! He won't be out for long."

Charlie was already out of the front door as Hetty scrambled down the ladder and ran out to sit on the man with Grace.

Charlie ran as fast as he could to the jetty and as luck would have it the ferry was in.

"Help Sam, we need rope. If we don't move quickly we will be in big trouble," Charlie called to the ferry boy. "Have you got any?"

"Yep, here you are, do you need help? What's going on?" Sam could see that Charlie was not messing around.

He jumped off the ferry and, grabbing a coil of rope, ran with Charlie back to the hut. As he got close to the hut he could see Grace and Hetty sitting on top of somebody.

"Tie him up quick Sam," said Charlie.

"Why, what has he done?"

"Just do it Sam, they will explain later!" ordered Grace.

Sam was so shocked to hear Grace complete a whole sentence that he quickly tied up the man's hands and feet.

"He won't get out of those knots in a hurry," boasted Sam.

Hetty tried to explain what was going on but she did not get very far before they heard in the distance the wail of sirens coming across the water.

"That sounds like the police launch," said Sam.

"Thank goodness, I'll go down to direct them," said Charlie and ran off.

Grace was sitting firm on the man who was clearly coming round and trying to move to a more comfortable position, spitting sand out of his mouth, coughing and spluttering. Bob was beside himself barking and jumping up and down for all he was worth, growling and sounding as fierce as he could.

"Well, who is he?" Sam asked as he pulled the knots tight and turned to look at Hetty as he helped Grace get to her feet.

"Oh my goodness!" Grace gasped "I'm too old for this type of excitement! What on earth is going on? Tell us who he is and what he's done."

In the distance the sirens were getting closer. Hetty helped Grace up the steps and started to explain about the children and that the man was actually their dad and that they were hiding from him inside the hut.

Hetty was opening the trapdoor and helping the children out when two policemen and a policewoman arrived following Charlie, who was panting as he tried to tell them what was happening.

"OK son, take a deep breath and take it slowly."

The tallest policeman looked around summing up the scene before them.

"I take it that this is Mr Osman and..." looking up at the veranda of the hut "...this must be Kaya and Hasan?"

'Smith' was still struggling and trying to escape from his bonds.

"Let me go!" he spluttered.

Hetty stepped forward, shielding the children from the sight of their father trussed up like a chicken on the sand below them.

"Well yes sir, that's what we think, the children are really frightened of him but he told us his name was Smith." Charlie was nodding in agreement and Grace just looked confused.

The policewoman came up the steps and guided the two children back into the hut with Hetty following.

"I'll look after the children in here and find out the story." She called back over her shoulder "Are you OK to sort things out here?"

"Yes fine, leave it to us." The two policemen started to untie Sam's ropes and replaced them with handcuffs.

Chapter 17

Hetty and the two children sat in the hut. The very kind policewoman introduced herself as WPC Caroline Jennings.

"You must be Hetty."

"Yes that's right and this is Kaya and Hasan. I'm really worried about Kaya, she is not very well. She feels really hot, is tired all the time and has not eaten much for a day now."

"Don't you worry now," said the policewoman. "We'll take both of them to hospital for a thorough check up."

Just at that moment the door opened and Dad put his head in, closely followed by Charlie and his grandparents.

"What on earth has been going on?" Dad looked from the policewoman to Hetty.

"Well, it's a long story, Dad." Hetty looked up at him trying to see what sort of mood he was in. He looked worried more than angry so Hetty introduced him to Hasan and Kaya and began to explain to him and the policewoman what had been going on during the past week.

"Well," said Dad. "I thought something was going on but I never expected this." He turned to the WPC "What happens now?"

"We need to take a statement at the police station Sir and you will need to come with Hetty and Charlie as a responsible adult unless Charlie's grandparents want to come as well." She looked at the adults. Charlie's grandparents looked concerned.

"I'll go, don't you two worry about it," said Dad.

A look of relief crossed Charlie's grandparents' faces.

Just at that moment a Land Rover arrived outside and out jumped a man and a lady in paramedic uniforms carrying a big rucksack each.

"We couldn't get the ambulance car here so Steve gave us a lift. Now, who is injured?"

WPC Jennings introduced the children and asked them to check Kaya.

"Has she been given any medication?" asked the paramedic.

"No, I thought about giving her a headache tablet but I was not sure if it was the right thing to do, so she hasn't had anything," explained Hetty.

"That was very sensible," the lady paramedic said to Hetty whilst taking Kaya's temperature. "We'll get back to the ambulance car and get them both to hospital to give them a thorough check-up. Well done both of you."

Hasan smiled at Hetty and Charlie sensing that he and his sister were safe now. He climbed into the backseat of the Land Rover whilst the paramedics lifted Kaya up to sit next to him. He turned to watch as his father was led away by the policemen with his hands tied behind his back.

"Do you think they will be alright Dad? They don't speak much English. Can't I go with them?" Hetty asked.

Dad looked at the state of the hut behind them. "I think we need to tidy up here before Sophie and Nigel get back," said Dad. "Will it be OK if we do that before we come to the police station and then we can go straight on to the hospital to check on Kaya and Hasan afterwards?" asked Dad, looking at Hetty, Charlie and the WPC.

"Yes, shall we say 2pm?" WPC Jennings asked.

"OK, two o'clock it is, Christchurch Police Station," said Dad

The police went back to the launch with Mr Osman who was still shouting. Hetty and Charlie took a policeman to the black hut, which was surrounded by police tape, and big signs warning people not to enter were erected.

Hetty, Dad and Charlie set to, to tidy and clean the hut ready for Sophie, Nigel and Jack's return. Luckily nothing was broken and soon it looked as good as new.

During lunch, Dad asked Hetty and Charlie lots of questions and as they answered he realised how brave they had been.

"I can't believe all this was going on and you did not say anything."

"Sorry Dad, I did not realise quite how nasty Mr Osman was." Hetty looked a bit tearful as she realised what a lucky escape they had had.

After lunch they set off for the police station. When they were settled in the interview room Hetty and Charlie again told their story and signed the statement at the end.

"Can we go to the hospital now? I really want to see how Hasan and Kaya are," implored Hetty.

"Are we done here?" asked Dad.

"Yes, thank you very much. If we have any further questions we will be in touch. You have both been very brave," said the WPC.

They drove to the hospital. As they reached the children's ward, the door opened and a very pretty lady came out escorted by another policewoman, followed closely by Hasan. He ran to Hetty and Charlie and hugged them. Then, holding their hands he pulled them over to the pretty lady who held her arms out to hug them as well.

"Thank you, thank you, for finding my babies!" She was laughing and crying at the same time "How can I ever repay you? Thank you with all my heart."

"How is Kaya? Where is she?"

"It looks like she has a bad infection, they have given her some antibiotics and she is looking better already," said Hasan's mum. "Come and see for yourselves."

Hetty and Charlie smiled at each other with relief.

"Thank goodness it wasn't anything serious." said Charlie.

* * *

Hetty, Dad and Charlie returned on the last ferry. "Well, what shall we do tomorrow?" asked Hetty grinning at Dad and Charlie.

Chapter 18

Saturday morning dawned bright and sunny; Hetty slept late and Dad let her have a lie in. The police were coming back at 11 o'clock so he made sure she was awake in time to have some breakfast. They called for Charlie and walked to the jetty to meet the same police officers who had interviewed them the previous afternoon.

As they walked people came out of their huts to wave, clap and cheer.

"Well done Hetty and Charlie," they called.

Several asked to take their photograph and shake their hands. Hetty and Charlie couldn't believe it; they felt like celebrities and grinned happily at everyone. Considering how worried and frightening parts of the last week had been Saturday felt like a new beginning.

The police arrived and they all went to the black hut. As they approached Hetty remembered being trapped inside and felt a bit panicky, Dad gave her a hug and Charlie winked at her, remembering his brave rescue bid.

After the police had searched the hut and removed various items of evidence, they asked to see the shed where the children were hidden when Hetty had found them.

As they walked with the police officers, Hetty and Charlie's story about the week together with what the police had been told by Mrs Osman made the story clearer.

The Osman family had lived in Turkey until the parents had decided to split up. Mum had decided to live in England with Kaya and Hasan, which Mr Osman was not happy about. He wanted them to live with him in his native country, Turkey, but their mum had defied him and had returned home to stay with her family in Bournemouth.

When they had lived in Turkey their father had only allowed them to speak Turkish, which explained why they hadn't understood Hetty very well. Their father had secretly followed them to England and tracked them down in Bournemouth. He then kidnapped the children intending to take them back to Turkey. He had hidden the children in the black hut, intending to keep them there until the fuss had died down and he could get them out of the country.

Bob had saved the day by finding the key to the hut and running off with it, leaving it unlocked for long enough for Hasan and Kaya to run away and hide in the old shed where Hetty had found them and the rest is history.

When they got back to Hetty's hut after the police had left, Dad stayed outside talking to a small crowd of people who had gathered outside.

When he eventually joined them inside he told Hetty and Charlie that there was going to be a party barbeque that evening.

"What for?" asked Charlie.

"Well for you two of course. It's at the café to celebrate the rescue and everyone is invited."

"Great, I can't wait, what time will it start?" asked Charlie.

"About 6.30 I think," said Dad.

"Hi," called a voice from outside the hut. "Excuse me but are Hetty and Charlie there?" The children opened the door and saw a woman dressed in jeans and a T-shirt with a camera slung around her neck. She had her right hand stretched out towards Dad.

"Hello, I'm Dee, from the local newspaper." As she shook hands with them all she indicated her camera. "Could I have a photograph and a few words, please? This is a great story, I love it, obviously you can't give too many details in case it goes to court but I'd love to have a picture for the paper next week, would that be OK?" She looked at Dad expectantly.

"Ooh Dad, can we?" said Hetty excitedly.

"Well I can't speak for Charlie, you'd have to ask his grandparents but I don't have any objections from Hetty's point of view. What it is to have a famous daughter!" he laughed.

As they went to see what Charlie's grandparents thought, Dad made some sandwiches, which they ate on the veranda after the journalist had finished taking her pictures.

Dad had checked Sophie and Nigel's hut earlier while Hetty was still asleep and was convinced that all was fine, which was just as well because at about three o'clock they arrived back. Dad decided that they ought to tell them about what had happened rather than them hear it from someone else.

"Oh my goodness!" exclaimed Sophie "What excitement and our little hut had a starring role, what a brave thing to do, can we come to the party as well?"

"Of course, everyone is invited and without your hut we may not have been able to rescue Hasan and Kaya." Hetty grinned at them and knelt down to tickle Jack.

Hetty yawned as she and Dad wandered back to their hut.

"Why don't you have a nap for an hour then you won't be too tired for the party this evening?" Dad suggested. He needed Hetty out of the way for a while; he had a surprise to arrange.

"Good idea, I am really tired for some reason." Hetty climbed up to her bed and fell asleep straight away.

Dad went outside and got on his phone.

At 6.30 exactly Dad, Hetty, Charlie, his grandparents and Lucy arrived at the café, led by Grace on her tricycle, parp-parping for all she was worth. Hetty gazed around, everyone seemed to be there. Megs, Ryan, Emily, Danni, Joe, Justin from The Beach House, WPC Jennings, the two paramedics, Sam the ferryboat boy, Mrs Osman, Hasan and an almost healthy-looking Kaya.

Hetty ran up and gave Kaya a hug.

"I am so pleased to see you, Kaya."

Everyone clapped as they walked into the crowd and started to sing very loudly.

"For they are jolly good fellows."

The chorus died away, followed by three cheers. The crowd parted, Hetty turned to see what everyone was looking at and couldn't believe her eyes, coming towards her being pushed in his wheelchair by Steve, the Land Rover man, was Grandpa, closely followed by Gran. Hetty ran towards them and as she was enveloped in a big hug from Grandpa she started to cry.

"How did you get here?" she sniffed as she wiped her eyes with a tissue that Gran gave her, as she too gave her a hug.

"Well, Dad arranged for Steve to come and pick us up as a surprise for you. You have been a very courageous girl and we are so proud of you." Gran smiled at her, wiping a little tear away as well.

"It wasn't just me Gran, Charlie was great and so was Grace and as for Bob...!"

She looked down at the little dog who was sitting at her feet looking as proud as punch; he knew who the real hero was.